M000040110

HALINE

SUNDEEP AHUJA

Forward Press Books

This is a work of fiction. All of the characters, organizations, events, objects, and places portrayed in this book are products of the author's imagination. Any resemblance to actual persons, living or dead, is purely coincidental.

HALINE © 2014 by Sundeep Ahuja
Published by Forward Press Books, 2014
All rights reserved.

FIRST PRINTING
ISBN: 978-0-9914312-1-2

haline.co
forwardpress.co

For those who understand the tenuous balance we have with Mother Earth and make choices that protect her.

Slava –

Brother. This book def would not have been possible without you –– especially since I crowdfunded it on your platform!

You have been an incredible friend and mentor... I deeply appreciate the love & support.

–

acknowledgements

Mom and Dad, thank you for unconditional, unwavering support and all the love in the world. Jasmeet, thank you for always believing in your brother.

Thanks also to the following family and friends for their help editing the novel: Mom and Dad, Jasmeet Ahuja, Brad Feldman, Parag Ladhawala, Tyler Willis, Ryan Troy, Satyender Mahajan, Shawn Bercuson, Kabir Sehgal, Raj Irukulla, Jeffrey Applebaum, Lauren Weinstein, Jaspaul Gogia, John Hering, Slava Rubin, Dev Dugal & Rajal Pitroda.

And to you, the reader: thank you for joining me in understanding the challenge ahead.

"It's too late. We're past the tipping point. Once the thermohaline flow shuts down, we can expect about twenty to thirty years of worst-case-scenario hell on Earth. God help us find our humanity on the other side."

— Spoken under condition of anonymity, twenty-nine years before Haline

"I remember a time, I remember it well,
before the haze of blistering days,
before the nightly cold spells.
I'd spend my time by the ocean's beaches
contemplating the shores she reaches,
wondering what they might teach us,
about the flow that touches each of us."

— From "The Lost Flow" published fourteen years before Haline

"We hereby establish this new republic and decree her to be called Haline—lest we forget our exploitive past, ensuring we remember to protect our future."

— President Gaven Jemmer's first-term acceptance speech,
first year of Haline

prologue

"We estimate about four dozen of them, sir!" Major Trey Benlin had to yell for his voice to be heard above the thumping rain. The smatter of gunfire up the ridge didn't help, nor did the thunder that rolled every five minutes. The storm was furious about something.

"Okay, Jemmer! Your team is to take out the militia. Don't pursue. Just get as many as you can, then have your drone squad push the rest past the perimeter-defense line and let our team out there do the rest. Split into two groups, one on the—"

Lightning flashed and Colonel Rylan Hawk paused for the expected rumble, his gray and black and wet beard glistening in the dim light. He continued loudly: "—on the rim of the dam, the other up this path here."

With his index finger, Rylan followed an incline on the holographic terrain map. Even under the tent nothing was dry, and the map phased and distorted as sideways-moving droplets from outside blew in. He looked up at Major Gaven

Jemmer, who stood suited in standard-issue military rain gear, hood pushed back, water running from his drenched hair down his wet face. "Understood?"

"Yes, sir!" Gaven nodded sharply.

"Benlin, even without these bastards trying to blow the dam, we have orders to reinforce the thing. There's an engineering team waiting at the bottom of the hill, here." He pointed again to the map. "We also have to make sure the desalination and decontamination equipment hasn't been sabotaged at the off chance their true objective was reservoir poisoning. Your team is to escort the engineers and do whatever it is they need you to do."

"Yes, sir. Understood." A streak of dripping mud ran along the left side of Trey's face. He didn't seem to notice.

Rylan took his fist off the table where he had been leaning over the map and stood up straight to face his top two Majors. He'd hand-selected them from dozens for the assignment knowing he could count on them, unlike the many others who were either too preoccupied with suffering borne by families back home, or worse—potentially traitorous.

"Gentlemen, these marauders think that with a few charges and some luck they can flood Center City and then come down and take what they want. Well, we're not going to let that happen."

He cracked the hint of a smile. "All right. Go get 'em!"

**

"Soel," Alyel whispered. In the background she heard the evening report broadcasting in the living room as the door to their apartment slid shut behind her. Leaning back, she closed her eyes, relaxed her shoulders, and indulged in a deep inhale.

It was not the long days of treating poisonous spider bites, acute malaria, advanced typhoid, sun burns, or frail bodies of the famished that she found most stressful.

"Violence that nature inflicts upon us after a millennium of us inflicting violence upon nature," she had once said to a nurse as she surveyed an overflowing waiting room filled with heavy faces at Central Hospital.

Rather, her stress was rooted in the twelve-minute walk between the emergency room at Central and the apartment she shared with her husband, Soel, four blocks away. Though the streets were regularly patrolled by city police, sometimes they themselves were the danger. Other times, especially as fall turned into winter, it seemed every alley she passed sheltered the hopeless and desperate—and hungry. If you were lucky they just wanted your keycard. Slightly less lucky, they would slit your wrists looking for hidden cardsafes. But in the cold, hunger trumped all other desires. If you were not lucky, your body was what they wanted.

So every day after work Alyel walked home with the shaky confidence that only the gun in her left jacket pocket could provide. Soel desperately wanted to escort her safely each evening, but her independent nature furiously protested. Each afternoon he walked alone, then, made dinner for them both, and sat in front of the living room screen, watching and waiting. He too worked at Central Hospital but at the opposite end of the two-block fortress of a building in the secretive GOD Department—Genetic Officer Development. He had slightly better hours and far better pay, but she got to keep her soul; it was a deal they struck when they were coming out of medical school together. Alyel again inhaled deeply, then walked into the living room.

"Hey, baby...come here, come look at this." Soel stared intently at the screen, eyes moist, lips quivering. "Look what they are doing now."

His face swiveled in her direction, and he stretched out a hand. "Sit with me."

Alyel fought the sudden desire to grab the lamp from the table next to Soel and throw it headlong at the screen. She ached to go back in time, before the wars. Instead, with the manic self-control she had honed over the past several years, she gently took her husband's hand and sat, kissed him on the cheek, then turned her head to see what his eyes saw.

A drenched field reporter stood outside a survival center in front of a line of raincoats and umbrellas that seemed to stretch for miles, his dronecam shuddering slightly in the strong wind as it broadcast:

Water levels have reached critical, stressing

*the levee structures and prompting the
president to preemptively declare a Federal
Disaster Area. Martial Law with a 2200
curfew for surrounding areas has also been
imposed. While locals remain hopeful the
actions will at least guarantee them
desperately needed food and water rations,
most expect little in the way of shelter.*

*Moments ago, the governor gave a press
conference seeking to quell fears in the
region that Congress would turn its back on
the mountain state and let it fall into the
hands of militia as happened to two coastal
states last year after similar flooding to the
west.*

The image moved from the tired reporter to the tired governor, a glaze in his eyes betraying the lack of sleep that his commanding voice sought to hide.

*I want you to know that engineers are
already working to reinforce the levees, and
as of now we don't believe an evacuation
will be necessary.*

His carefully chosen words were read off the screen to the left of the camera in measured cadence, his eyes dashing from the audience, to his script, and back.

*To address the food situation, while it is true
that the rains and floods have spoiled a
portion of our reserves, we have been
preparing for this contingency for some
time, and there are no expected shortages.*

Stressing the word "no," the governor paused, seemingly expecting applause or nods of support. He of course got nothing.

> *Finally, our walls, fences, and defenses to the north and south are holding, and President Renton has assured me he will provide additional troops if needed. What's most important is that residents know that we will not fail them and that we have the full support of the president.*

The governor leaned forward, put his hands on both sides of the podium, and looked deep into the camera. "We will not fail you."

He paused again, an expression of defeat peeking through his makeup. "Let us bow our heads in prayer…"

The news turned to images of people in an affected area where floods had already wreaked havoc: a family of four, the girl on her mother's shoulders, the boy on his father's, fording a river-street; a couple standing in each other's arms alone on a rooftop island as water moved debris and bodies around them; masked looters breaking into a third-floor jewelry shop, piling their plunder into a waiting speedboat; a golden retriever delicately balancing on top of what was once a streetlamp as it was slowly enveloped. The voice of the reporter was drowned out by the disbelief that engulfed Alyel. Her brain processed the tragedy and failure, her heart the pain and fear.

Soel motioned the screen off. Alyel found her left hand covering a gaping mouth and her right hand tightly gripping Soel's arm, whose right hand was lightly placed on her softly protruding belly bump. They sat there in silence, holding on.

**

"With all due respect, those days are over and there is *no* going back. When the ocean died most of our markets died with it. Sir, you heard the pundits as to what happens next. It's only going to get worse."

Venka paused for a response, and to catch her breath. She was taking a risk being so young making a prediction so bold, but risks like this were exactly what had earned her the CEO's ear.

She took his silence as her cue to continue: "In order to survive we'll have to consolidate and collaborate. There's no other way. Either we have peaked and from here falter and fail, disappearing into oblivion, or we look at this as an opportunity."

She leaned in. "Sir, we own the resources. We have the capital. All we need is a plan."

part one

1

"Ladies and gentlemen, I present you SAI—Sentient Artificial Intelligence. The culmination of years of work that began before the wars and continued amid the fighting, she is supreme in her abilities, vast in her knowledge, and—most of all—committed to the safety and prosperity of Haline. Consider her your new best friend who will be by your side, everywhere and always."

— President Gaven Jemmer, SAI unveiling event, second year in office

YEAR 6 OF HALINE, FOUR DAYS UNTIL ELECTION
EARLY EVENING, GAMMA RING

On his way home from the office Joaquin stopped by the neighborhood store to pick up the groceries Lyla had ordered. Lyla, who seemed as certain about him as she was about the color of the sky. How could she be so sure? But he appreciated her companionship. And her smile. And, of course, her patience. He wasn't sure what love was, but he wondered if it was what he felt when he held her.

Walking into the store, his relatively tall frame drew the attention of a middle-aged woman as she searched through the poor selection of rotting orsoy vegfruits. A genetic cross between oranges and soy beans, orsoys had been engineered for a combination of calories, nutrition, and durability, with a shelf life of six months. These had been sitting in Alpha longer before being sent to Gamma. She squinted her eyes as if to focus them, decided he was no one special, and went back to her search.

The screens in each corner of the store broadcast the latest Election news. The young female reporter was reminding everyone of the increased fines for Election boycotters—Cotters, they were called—this year, with the subtlest tone of condescension. A small part of her audience was like her: living in the Alpha or Beta Rings, privileged, civilized, loyal. But the masses she spoke to in the outer Rings were *not* like her and needed to be reminded.

Joaquin made his way through a disheveled aisle of packaged food rations to the produce pick-up area in the back, passing the three-days-new security guard, who once again—as he had the two days prior—eyed him suspiciously. The guard's hands sat on his waist, his right fingers inches from his private security-class minmax gun as if hoping Joaquin would try something. Seemingly on cue, the reporter switched to a story about rising produce theft in the Gamma, Delta, and Epsilon Rings. Joaquin walked up to the counter, offering a half smile to Tommas.

"No one's stealing your lousy produce, are they, Tomm?" he said, waving the inside of his right wrist over the counter-embedded scanner, getting a monotone "*Joaquin Deva, order 42719, payment accepted,*" in reply.

"With ugly customers like you to scare them away?" Tommas replied, wryly. "Nah, it's pretty quiet 'round here. Couple miles up the road though…" His grizzly voice and thick beard matched his dark expression, and he finished his sentence with a slight shake of his head. Then his deep-set eyes caught something new. "What's that on your wrist there?"

He'd forgotten he was wearing it. Unfastening the strap, Joaquin placed the device on the counter as carefully as if he were putting down an heirloom zucchini. "It's called a 'watch.' It tells time, and folks used to wear these things around the outside of their wrists. Fascinating, right?"

Joaquin looked up for a reply, and getting nothing, he turned his right wrist over. Glowing lightly were the digits: "18:02:51." The last two digits ticked forward: "52," "53."

Tommas's eyes looked curiously at the black, oddly shaped device, and he replied detachedly, sadly, as if his mind were somewhere painful. "Yeah, fascinating..."

He disappeared behind the steel-reinforced wall between the front part of the store and the Produce Safety & Storage area in the back to fetch Joaquin's order. At the doorway stood another security guard, hands on belt and attention on the broadcast.

Joaquin turned around and leaned his elbows onto the counter. Glancing upward toward the screen, he caught the unflinching eyes of a young, slight girl in pigtails and pink overalls, holding her mother's hand absentmindedly. There was really nothing out of the ordinary about Joaquin's outward appearance that merited the locked stare; dark khaki trousers with the sheen of a fresh sunproof wash, a sky-blue collared shirt with the same sheen, and deep-brown canvas loafers were all pretty standard Haline Gamma-class government-employee attire. He wondered if it was the watch, but assumed it was the usual—at six foot three he was taller than most in the Gamma Ring and occasionally (or was it often?) attracted curious eyes, especially those of curious children.

Hearing a rustling behind him, Joaquin turned back around. After another half smile and nod to Tommas as he took his purchase, Joaquin walked outside with the groceries in a light mesh bag slung across his chest and over his left shoulder, a one-gallon flexsteel canister of purified drinking water held firmly in his right palm.

The warm November evening with its setting sun and rising moon carried a crispness that touched his skin with a calming energy. He stopped and inhaled. Closed his eyes. Held the moment in his lungs. Exhaled. At this altitude he could never seem to get enough of it—never *quite* fill his lungs entirely. Rarely did a deep breath seem deep enough to give him that feeling of satisfaction he remembered from days by the ocean in his youth, but he often tried.

Joaquin opened his eyes and glanced at the brightly lit T-bus stop across the street—four minutes, fourteen seconds until the next one. If he waited he'd be home in only eleven minutes *and* avoid the mosquitoes that roamed each dusk in search of feast. But with another deep, not-quite-fulfilling breath, Joaquin turned on his heel and started the twenty-three minute walk home. Glancing under his wrist, he saw he had another 442 calories to burn before he hit his Haline-mandated, personalized goal of 2,712 minimum calories burned for the day, and he remembered Lyla despised after-dinner strolls; she didn't feel safe in his Gamma neighborhood, despite the roving scout patrols. *Or perhaps because of them?* Besides, the mosquitoes usually spared him, and he could use the time to ponder the old uses of his new toy.

EARLY EVENING, BETA RING

Lieutenant Aaren Jemmer arrived back at police headquarters, and the exhausted yet joyful smile of a productive day gave way to a blank expression that reflected the loneliness that awaited him at home. He unsnapped his hard-body chest gear as he made his way to the changing room, exchanging hellos and salutes with fellow officers and staff he passed in the hall. On the screen he noticed the ongoing coverage of the upcoming Election.

> *The president is confident that the people will reward his success in maintaining stable food supplies and doubling personal security initiatives with another term.*
>
> *Though there were expectations that the Cotters would wage an unprecedented propaganda war this Election, the improving conditions in the Gamma, Delta, and Epsilon*

> *Rings have eroded much of their support.*
> *Decreased attacks from Latmero and warm*
> *relations with our suppliers have further*
> *bolstered his position. When elected, it will*
> *be the third consecutive term for President*
> *Jemmer.*

The smile returned to Aaren's face as it often did when he heard his last name preceded by the word "president." "Jemmer" was a safe family name during the wars that regained popularity with the rise of now-President Gaven Jemmer. He eased his chest gear over his head and slipped on a light jacket, wondering what a third term for President Jemmer would mean for Lieutenant Jemmer. An easier life, probably, given the ever-increasing authority and control the president seemed to command, resulting in greater public safety and dwindling Resistance and Cotter movements. Fine by him. The Resistance had already all but disappeared, and the Cotters didn't seem to pose much of a threat anymore.

Sitting down, he snapped off his officer boots and slipped on his street shoes, taking a second to appreciate the way they felt on his worn feet—light, airy, comfortable. It was a feeling he always enjoyed after a long day—but one he treated as a reward more than a right, for reasons he kept carefully to himself. He picked up a boot and ran his fingers over the red stitch of the Haline emblem: six concentric rings and a blocky *H* stretching from the top of the outer ring to its bottom. He stood and put it in his locker along with its pair, then turned to watch the screen for a few seconds before mumbling, "See you at home, SAI," and taking the lift down to the garage.

_____

EVENING, EPSILON RING

Natasha muted the screen in frustration. She was just over three days away from the Election, and she still had nothing.

"This is your last chance, Natasha. Your *last chance*." She closed her eyes and rubbed her temples. Breathing, whispering, thinking. "Last chance…last chance…last chance."

Natasha walked to the mirror in the makeshift ready-room and looked at herself, seeing the familiar face of disappointment.

"Last chance, Natasha. If he wins by the margin he wants there's no telling what he'll do. Failure is not an option." But even as she uttered the words she knew them to be false; as of right now, failure looked to be the inevitable option. Again.

She stood for a moment, then grabbed her acid rain–proof olive-khaki jacket from the coat rack in the corner and walked down the tunnel toward the surface exit for some fresh air. Perhaps the twilight sky would have her answer. Emerging silently into the deserted park, Natasha quietly closed the gate behind her and moved to the fenced grove of willow trees. The air always smelled a bit better, a bit *fuller*, by those trees. She slowly closed her senses to the sounds of crickets and buzzing night insects and opened them to the quarter moon smiling down on her, almost mockingly.

"What does it really matter? Everyone's safer now. Let go and move on…" She said softly to the night sun, and to anyone who dared be out past Epsilon Ring curfew. But the silence of the evening echoed back, unconvinced by her tone, and the moon's unwavering expression reflected what she feared, what she knew most deeply: of course it mattered. Now more than ever, perhaps.

Loosening the snaps on her boots, she sank to the ground and leaned back against a rock. Natasha turned her eyes downward to the uncut blades of wild grass wafting back and forth in the soft wind, her legs outstretched and crossed at the feet, her arms folded across her chest. She inhaled slowly, closing her eyes to meditate. *Now more than ever.*

2

"Our forefathers almost lost all food-bearing crops to the sulfuric acid rains they themselves caused by spraying sulfate aerosols into the atmosphere in order to reduce the effects of climate change. Though these rains continue today, we are fortunate to have negotiated preferred terms with our neighbors to the south who are gifted with better weather and bountiful fields of produce. With these agreements, we expect to comfortably exceed demand in the coming years. I give daily thanks to have such generous partners as we heal as a people and as a country."

— President Gaven Jemmer, Second State of the Union, first term

SAME DAY
EVENING, GAMMA RING

As his apartment door slid open Joaquin realized Lyla had beaten him home. It had only been two days since he'd authorized her to his flat, and he instinctively tensed at the unfamiliar sound of someone in his kitchen. In his eight years since graduating from college he'd never had a roommate, and in all his twenty-nine years he'd never had a real girlfriend—let alone one who had access to his flat—but he needed to get past that. Joaquin relaxed and smiled at the prospect of Lyla in his apartment before he got home every evening. It felt good.

"Hi, honey," he jingled as he walked into the kitchen. Joaquin lifted the mesh bag of groceries over his head and placed it onto the table, setting the water canister down next to it. He came up behind her at the sink where she was sanitizing the dishes, humming quietly yet cheerily along with the pop tune playing softly on the panel radio. At the touch of his hands on her waist she jumped, and for a split second the glass in her hand was lost to gravity before she caught it and whipped around.

"Joaquin! I didn't hear you…for God's sake, don't ever do that again. I thought you were…just…"

"C'mon Lyla, really? Like you have to worry about anything. The moment anyone recognized you?" Who would dare mess with the congressional leader's daughter? Not even the police. Not yet, anyway.

"Yeah well, I worry. Not everyone likes my broadcasts." She sighed and turned her eyes to the table. "Ah, thank you for getting the groceries." She put the glass down and gave Joaquin a quick want-to-be-angry-at-you-but-I'm-not-really glance before making her way over to the mesh bag.

"You know how much I hate the store. What's that on your wrist?"

"Huh? Oh." Joaquin looked down, again forgetting he was wearing it. "It's called a watch. It tells time, and people used to wear it *outside* their wrist. Fascinating, right?"

Lyla unfastened the bag and began carefully taking out each item for inspection.

"Yeah, but not as fascinating as these vegmos. I swear, beta-carrots are getting smaller every day. And this c-bell pepper...it's the size of a tangberry." Her mildly disgruntled tone matched her bent eyebrows and frowning lips.

"Well, at least we have carrots and c-bells, Lyla." Joaquin turned his head to stare out the window of his kitchen into his neighbor's window in the adjacent building. The older, fatigued woman he often saw there this time of evening stood sanitizing dishes as he'd expected.

"I saw a girl today at the store. She couldn't have been more than five, all skin and bones. Her mother was grazing..." His voice trailed off, and he turned to Lyla. "I wonder how she'll grow up, you know?"

"That's not our problem, Joaquin." Lyla's mild frustration became mildly more severe as she evaluated the petite, genetically modified vegetables laid out in front of her. "Right now, our problem is how you and I are going to grow up. This'll barely be enough for a proper dinner, and I know they charged you more than last time." She shook her head. "We'll have to place a bigger order next time. Again."

Joaquin heard her, but his eyes turned back out the window to the woman, and his thoughts strayed back to the girl at the store.

EVENING, BETA RING

Lieutenant Aaren Jemmer pressed his thumb on the entry pad and opened the slide door to his flat. The table was set—dinner for one—and the warm, pungent smell of garlic told Aaren he had just missed the delivery. Turning the corner into the kitchen, the screen displayed the menu and the time of drop off: chicksoy gravy with mushrooms and potatoes, three minutes, thirty-two seconds ago. Aaren tapped the transceiver around his ear: "SAI, Aaren Jemmer removing trans."

"Acknowledged, Lieutenant Aaren Jemmer," SAI replied in her sultry, commanding yet gentle voice out of the transceiver—and from the screen in the main room.

SAI—ever present in every citizen's ear, every citizen's home, every citizen's life. As a senior officer, Aaren was authorized to disconnect from SAI from time to time, and always when off duty—one of the small perks of service that doubled as a way for the government to avoid having evidence of or being complicit in off-duty indiscretions. She was friendly and helpful most times, but could be ruthless if you ever found yourself on the wrong side of her enforcement of Haline laws—some say as programmed by the president himself.

Aaren placed the small transceiver on the counter. Off came his officer-class minmax gun from his belt, the belt itself, and his gloves. He unsnapped his street shoes, eased them off his feet, and went into the ready-room where he soaped his hands and moved them under the faucet. A gentle but thick stream of water flowed for precisely seven seconds. Aaren wiped his hands on the towel, grabbed a water ration, and popped the anti-spore pill that sat waiting for him on the counter. *I wonder why they didn't engineer officers to be immune to spore infection?* He smiled. *Not that it mattered.*

Swallowing the pill, Aaren took out his dinner from the oven where it was kept to stay warm, and moved to the couch where the screen instantly turned on to broadcast the country's national channel, HN, with the latest Election coverage.

> *President Jemmer, who runs unopposed this Election year, is hoping for eighty percent of the vote—eighteen percent more than the previous Election—and asks each of you for your support. This is a speech given earlier today on the steps of the presidential bunker.*

The screen moved from the polished reporter to the polished President Gaven Jemmer, standing over six feet tall but seeming nearly eight above the thousands of citizens before him on the steps in front of Bunker One.

> *Friends and fellow citizens of Haline, you have humbled me with your support these past six years, and with it I have strived to serve you.*
>
> *The world that left us with little water and less food after ending the life-giving thermohaline flow and starting life-taking floods, the world that left us in war with our neighbors and friends, mistrusting and wary of the disease we each might carry, the*

> *world where the desperate killed brothers*
> *and sisters for food—that world is behind*
> *us.*

The crowd of well-dressed Alphas and Betas erupted into applause. *They are the lucky ones, and they applaud the man who keeps them lucky*, Aaren mused, taking another bite of his dinner. He'd seen enough to not be naive about that anymore.

> *Our nation of Haline, with a population now*
> *approaching six million, has—with your*
> *sacrifice and support—come together to*
> *create a new flow. A flow of law and*
> *security that feeds and provides water for*
> *every citizen, protects the health of every*
> *citizen, and ensures the safety of every*
> *citizen in this life and the next.*

More cheers. Slight head shake. Another bite.

> *Our enemies have tried everything,*
> everything *to make us weak, but their*
> *sanctions, blockades, and attacks are no*
> *match for our determination, our ingenuity,*
> *and our courage. My fellow Halinites, allow*
> *me to continue to lead us toward a*
> *prosperous future and I will deliver you to it!*

The applause was thick, and the cameras began focusing on individual faces of the well-fed and fit leaders of the country. A confident Vice President Ginara Martin. A squirrely Defense Secretary Kip Rogan. A nervous

Congressional Leader Danyela Clarek. *Yes, of course she's nervous…she's becoming irrelevant.*

Aaren motioned the screen off and finished the rest of his dinner in contemplative silence. *What would a third term look like for me…*

_____

LATE EVENING, EPSILON RING

Natasha heard a rustling and opened her eyes to see Adler emerge from the ground gate. Upon stepping out, he too looked up into the unusually clear night sky with its bright half moon and stood a moment before walking over and sitting down next to her. He was silent, then spoke softly: "The team was just watching a recap of his address."

"And?" Natasha asked, eyes closed again, uninterested in the expected reply.

"And…it was pretty good, Natasha. He's leaving nothing to chance even with his popularity where it is." Adler let out a defeated sigh. "Xander, Ambrose, and Teena tendered their resignations after the broadcast and left with their things. They wanted to say goodbye but…they had everything ready and didn't want to—"

"It's his job." Natasha ignored the news of more of her troops giving up the fight—giving up on her—and focused on the only thing that would justify her years of struggle and grant her victory: engineering a popular boycott of the Election.

"And of course he's leaving nothing to chance. If he wins this Election unopposed and with support from eighty percent of Halinites he might never need to run again."

Adler opened his mouth as if to say something but changed his mind, keeping silent. Natasha opened her eyes and looked up at the half moon. She waited a long moment before continuing.

"My mother was a senator. Did I ever tell you that?"

"No...I had no idea." Adler's look of surprise gave way to a chuckle. "Natasha, you barely talk at all about yourself. Some on the team wonder if you were sent here during the wars from some other underground in some other country."

Natasha smiled at that.

"I was born here, long before it became Haline, of course." She threw Adler an amused glance. Perhaps she should be more open with her team. At least, perhaps, with Adler.

"Both my parents were serving at the time, my mother as a senator and my father as a district judge. I even had—" she stopped suddenly. "Or maybe I still have," she continued a second later, "an older brother. Eleven years older." Natasha caught Adler's expression out of the corner of her eye and laughed, giving him a knowing smile of embarrassed acknowledgement.

"Yes, I probably was a surprise, but my parents embraced me with love. My brother left for boarding school when I was only two. I never saw or heard from him again."

Natasha sat up a bit, pulling her jacket closer around her. At Haline's altitude, the nights cooled quickly.

"I was nine when my mother died. Transport accident." She paused, remembering. "But as I stood at the doorway, trying to understand what the police chief was telling my father, I didn't believe him." She turned to look at Adler, to see his eyes. "You remember what it was like back then."

"Yes…yes I do." Adler's mind visited his own mental closet where he stashed away his painful, pre-Haline memories. He remembered his father, deported for being of foreign birth when he was only seven. His mother, killed that very morning when they came to take his father away for standing in the way of the soldiers. His baby sister, all he had left in the world, taken from him the next day as the provisional government commandeered their property and sent the two children to two separate orphanages.

"*For your own good, son. You'll thank us later,*" the marginally official-looking officer had said as he opened drawers and cabinets in the house looking for valuables to pocket before taking them away.

Feeling his chest tighten, Adler started coughing, and he took out his ozone balancer. He inhaled from it then lightly shook the flashback from his head.

"My father died eleven years later, when I was twenty. Mugging." Natasha looked down at her feet. "I didn't think that was an accident either."

"I'm sorry, Natasha."

Natasha waited to reply.

"It was Julian who told me they had both been killed by the people who put Jemmer into power. At first I didn't want to believe him, part of me hoping he was making it up just to recruit me to join the Cotters, but...he had proof."

"Natasha, I had no idea—"

"I tell myself I'm fighting in the light of their legacy of justice, living a life that would have made them proud. But I sometimes wonder if I'm not trying to somehow avenge their deaths." Natasha paused, picking at her boots.

"Adler...why are we fighting if people are truly safer now than back then, during the wars? If my parents were alive today the worst that could happen is three, maybe six years imprisonment if they were activists about anything, right? But at least I would get to see them."

Adler felt ashamed that a part of him agreed. Passionately. *If my parents were alive today...*

Natasha inhaled sharply as emotion crept into her voice. She refocused before continuing. "But the Haline of tomorrow won't look anything like the Haline of today, will it. Just like the Haline of today looks nothing like its first year. Safer but at what cost?"

Natasha turned to look again at Adler—her lieutenant, her adviser, and, she realized in that moment, her only friend. "Outside of a dead Resistance and weak Congress we're the only ones who will do anything about it. We have work to do, Adler. Let's go."

"There's one more thing, Natasha." Adler reached his hand out to Natasha's shoulder to keep her seated and sat up to kneel so he could speak facing her directly. Now was the moment to tell her.

"It's about Congress, actually. Hidek just got back from meeting with his contact in Alpha. He has reason to believe that if reelected..." Adler was afraid to finish his sentence. "Natasha, the president intends to revoke congressional authority...to effectively dissolve Congress."

"What?" Natasha sat up with the energy of an electric shock through every one of the one hundred trillion cells in her body.

"How? The people won't...he can't, according to the Constitution, which means the police won't—"

"Hidek's source believes the president is confident he legally *can*, and has found a way to make it acceptable. Something about leveraging divisions in Congress and public dissatisfaction with elected officials to turn it into an economic issue on the back of a popular vote—this Election's popular vote—so he can claim it as a mandate *from* the people. Natasha..."

Adler sat down again, facing her. "Hidek's source has it that, on Election Day, the president will publicly claim that Congress is broken and should no longer be funded. He'll then announce an intention to channel the savings into cheaper food rations to make the maneuver more than agreeable."

"The people won't stand…" Even as they left her lips, Natasha lost faith in her own words.

"Won't they, Natasha?"

She turned her head away and then back, staring intently into Adler's eyes and seeing unquestioned belief in his every word. Hidek's sources and intelligence had most always proved sound, unfortunate as it often was.

Dissolve Congress! Natasha didn't dare try to comprehend the consequences. A notion that would have led to nationwide rioting just three years ago now sounded like not just a possible future, but a probable one.

"If that happens, we're through." Without congressional blessing as an underground political party, the Cotters would be no more than another faction of the Resistance. *But that would be just the beginning.*

She shook her head and continued, "Adler, without a Congress…Jemmer will raise food prices, ration anti-spore pills, bring back shock monitoring…" Natasha spoke the words as if resigned to their inherent, inevitable truth.

"He'll force through his Retirement Bill." Preemptive euthanasia. The implications of it all made her dizzy.

"I haven't told anyone. And I've asked Hidek to keep this to himself for now." Adler looked to his leader with eyes of shame as if this were his fault. As messenger, the burden of his message and its consequences weighed deeply on him.

Natasha forced her muscles to relax and slowly sat back against the rock, her eyes returning to the ground by her feet. She shook a possible future from her head to focus on her definite present; for now, she still had time. But try as she might, she'd been unsuccessful at rallying a movement with any argument against the president or his policies. Among the constantly improving conditions of the Alpha and Beta residents, she had no case. Amid the deteriorating conditions of the outer Rings, fear trumped any desire to fight. And now it was too late. *Unless…*

Natasha closed her eyes and inhaled as her thoughts coalesced around a singular truth: in the three days she had until Election, she needed something that discredited and undermined not the policies of the man but the man himself. Something material and irrefutable that would spread from citizen to citizen like a wildfire beyond containment. Natasha had one more shot, and it couldn't be merely wounding. It needed to be fatal.

A rumble and flash in the distance roused her from her meditation, and she looked to the west at a gathering darkness that blotted out the stars. "C'mon, let's go in." Natasha stood, dusted herself off, then extended an arm to Adler to help him up. "You're not wearing a jacket."

3

"Security is not free; we learned that the hard way during the wars. Unfortunately, security demands a hefty price we all must be willing to pay if we all want to benefit from its sheltering umbrella. Thus, when a minor personal freedom is sacrificed to preserve our major collective freedom, that is dear but necessary payment. And honoring that cost is true patriotism."

— President Gaven Jemmer's speech before Congress
upon the passage of the Safety Act

—————————

THREE DAYS UNTIL ELECTION
EARLY MORNING, GAMMA RING

Joaquin stands on a ridge overlooking the shimmering blue enormity of the ocean, which runs as far into the distance as he can fathom. He's filled with dueling senses of awe and fear, as if there's something he doesn't quite understand about it but he feels he must. Squinting his eyes to make out the horizon where the ocean meets the sky, Joaquin marvels at how impossibly far it seems. Below him, he hears the waves crashing against the rocks...calm yet violent, periodic yet urgent. The sheer wonder of it all wins out, and turning to look up, he asks, "Uncle, can we get closer?"

His uncle's head glows in the shining sun, the tiniest beads of sweat collecting on his brow. Joaquin knew the answer before he asked the question but is still disappointed with his uncle's slowly shaking head, his eyes fixated on the water. "We can't, Joaquin...but remember this, just as it looks now...not a still-threatening disaster of our past, but a beautiful and bountiful offering for our future, not to be feared but understood."

The chimes from his transceiver grew louder, stirring Joaquin from his sleep. He opened his eyes to a world where the ocean was a thousand miles away and creeping ever closer. "I'm awake, SAI."

He sat up with a deep breath, stretched his long arms, and looked over at Lyla. She lay delicately asleep on her side, facing him, her brown hair poured across the pillow, her face a tranquil glow. In moments like this he was gripped by an inexplicable desire to be with her at all times and for all time, but this morning that feeling was contrasted with a burning curiosity.

Has she seen the ocean? With her own eyes? he wondered. *Probably not,* he quickly decided, remembering their conversations about what it was like for her during the wars. He remembered the title her mother held. *Definitely not.*

He stared at her with warmth, just one more second, before sliding quietly out of bed toward the ready-room to begin his morning.

"Come back here."

Joaquin turned to see Lyla stretching her arms and hands toward him, her face in a yawn.

"Morning, sunshine." He bent to give her a kiss.

"I was just having the most intense dream. About this damn Election. I dreamt..." she paused, the images and feelings slipping away. She struggled to hold on.

"I dreamt that my mom was elected president. Isn't that funny?"

"Lyla, SAI..." Joaquin whispered.

"It was a dream, come on...those aren't illegal yet, are they? I saw my mom as a write-in candidate, winning, and for some reason, it wasn't a surprise. To the people, I mean. It was like everyone expected it..."

Joaquin paused and admired Lyla. She had a depth about her he was only beginning to understand. "What do you think it means?"

"I think it means..." Lyla smiled and put her arms around him, "that you should take the day off and we should start our vacation now."

Joaquin closed his eyes and sat in her embrace a moment, but his mind chased the echo of her words. "How is your mom? She okay with everything? The Election and all?"

Lyla paused a moment before replying. "Yeah, she's been a bit distant lately...I dunno what it is. I'm sure she's fine but..." Lyla sat up, propping a pillow behind her, staring. "She likes that I'm spending more time with you."

"Yeah?" Joaquin instinctively sat up straighter.

"Yeah...she says you remind her of my father. Which I guess you kind of do, from what I can remember."

In his mind's eye Joaquin compared himself to what he had heard about her deceased father, a rising star in the pre-Haline government—until he was assassinated. "Well, I'll take that as a compliment."

"Like mother, like daughter, I guess, huh?" She finished the last words in another yawn.

"Yeah...but I like that you stay out of the spotlight. It means I get more of you to myself." Joaquin pulled Lyla against him for a lingering kiss.

An hour later he was at the office, where the mood was light and borderline jovial—four days off for the Election, starting tomorrow.

"So, Joaquin, got any big plans for the holiday?" He turned to see Han just a few steps behind him. Han was his neighbor, his confidant, his friend. At five feet, eleven inches, Han was average height for a Halinite, but his browner skin always caused hesitation on first encounters—was he loyal? The thought that anyone would question Han always made Joaquin tense up in mild anger. Wasn't he born and raised here like everyone else? Hadn't his Alpha-class work on communication protocols helped keep the country safe? Han was more than loyal. Plus, he was a bona fide genius.

"I'm sure Lyla has some plans for us, but if it were up to me I'd check out a couple books from the restricted list and disappear for a few days."

Joaquin's reply was heavier than he intended. He was looking forward to spending time with Lyla, but missed being alone. He forced a smile. "How about you? Got any plans with Gail?"

"Nah, we broke up last night." Han paused. "Rather, she broke up with me. Yeah, that's what happened, let's be honest." He slipped into the kitchenette to buy a spinapple from the produce vendmac, swiping his wrist above the scanner and then making his selection. Joaquin took the moment to notice the rows and rows of mostly empty cubes, as many of his government colleagues took an extra day off to get out of town, probably to the Zeta Ring. *Wouldn't that be a nice vacation.*

"Maybe I'll steal your idea...Lord knows I need the distraction. Four days alone in my flat and I'm liable to kill myself." Han was back, spinapple in hand and partially in mouth. "But instead of the restricted list, I'll probably pick something up at the store."

Joaquin turned his head to meet Han's glinting eyes, and they both smiled. Oh, the store, where Han met Gail. And Shyla before her. And Abbi before her. And...well, the list went on.

"Anyway, see you for lunch." Han took a left in the direction of the Network Communications Department, leaving Joaquin to walk the thirty remaining feet to the security door of the Archives Room.

Suited up, Aaren felt he was born an officer. Specialty black boots, heavy enough for any terrain yet light enough to sprint in. Dark mesh pants designed to withstand casual knife swipes, yet breathable to prevent overheating, and with a built-in cooling system. His minmax-shield hard-body vest over his dark mesh shirt, his minmax belt, and minmax gun. And his favorite—an officer-class dashglass. He arrived in a good mood at the front of the store, where a Cotter was spotted just hours earlier. "SAI, show me the two minutes before and after Adler was here today."

His dashglass darkened and displayed a frame of the front of the store as captured by a surveillance camera across the street. It began playing at double speed, highlighting the names of the citizens that came and went through the field of vision. Nothing out of the ordinary as he looked for—there, Adler Loran. "Pause SAI. Play back ten-s prev in slow."

Adler barely passed through the camera field, clearly attempting to avoid identification. He picked up something dropped by…"SAI, show me the store view thirty-s prev to incident and run scan for Karl Porto."

Just as he finished the command, through his darkened dashglass he saw a boy dart out of the store and cut right down the street in a full run. "SAI, halt search and normalize."

The dashglass lens lightened as Aaren took off in pursuit. "Son, there's no point in running," Aaren yelled out after the boy, one foot darting out after the other, his hands cutting back and forth by his sides. The boy's head whipped around, shocked to hear anyone after him. Seeing an officer, he picked up speed, dodging the confused, sun-hatted, a-jacket-clad crowd in the street just out doing their morning pre–Election vacation shopping.

"Would you like a scout, Officer Jemmer?" SAI offered in his ear, monitoring the situation.

"No, I can handle it." Many officers relished use of SAI-commanded drones, or "scouts," any chance they could. About the size and shape of two large fists, scouts were one part surveillance, one part killing machines. Never sure who had ultimate control, however, him or SAI, Aaren avoided using them whenever possible.

"Really, kid, not worth running. Spare your parents the embarrassment." Aaren's bellowing voice thinned as it made its way through the noise of the crowd, but he was sure the boy still heard him.

It was always harder identifying children as they weren't required to wear transceivers—the people had stood up for that—but there was usually enough of a record to identify them if they were the troublesome sort. An unfortunate downside of the "T-13" law—plotting adults had begun finding kids under thirteen to do their dirty work for them. Alas, this was probably one of those cases.

"SAI, map from CL, three-block R." *Let's see where you're going.*

His dashglass projected a translucent, moving map five feet in front of his face. The boy turned a corner into an alley away from the main street and then began to slow. Aaren closed the gap quickly as the boy came to a stop and turned around.

"Ah...you just needed to put on a show for whoever put you up to this." Aaren walked the last few steps, catching his breath, until he was within a few feet of the boy. He pushed the button on the left arm of his dashglass to capture all aspects of the scene before taking it off. Then he pushed a button just above his left wrist that released a cooling mist beneath his sweltering suit, immediately soothing him. Aaren glanced at the inside of his right wrist: 108 degrees of saturating heat where he was standing now.

"No." The boy was sweating and panting, but his answer was firm. In his left hand he gripped a bulging canvas bag, likely filled with vegmos and vegfruits.

"I stopped because I'm done running." With a grunt the boy gripped the bag with both hands and swung it over the fence, where a rustle exposed an accomplice who took off into the adjacent park.

Clever. Aaren was somewhat impressed and yet saddened that his original hypothesis about the boy being used was likely wrong. He wiped the sweat off his forehead with his shirt cuff. "You should have given me that bag. Now I have to take you in. I could have gone easy on you."

"If I had given it back my brothers would starve in days." For a young boy he had a visceral anger in his eyes, and that anger—on behalf of his brothers? Or perhaps caused by missing parents?—was directed squarely at Aaren. For a moment, Aaren felt as if he were the one who should be afraid.

"But what do you care? Do what you will with me."

They stood there, the two of them—the boy ready to bear the punishment of imprisonment for stealing, and the officer in charge of monitoring the boycotters distracted by a kid who just wanted to feed his brothers. Homeless and helpless.

"SAI, off for five." With a tap to just behind his left ear they were alone. Aaren crouched down to level with the boy.

"Do you know where any of the Cotters are? If you tell me, or even give me a hint, I'll let you go."

"Ha!" The boy even had the sarcasm of an adult. "Like I'd tell you. Every time I hit a store—"

"So this isn't your first time—"

"I know I'll eventually get caught." The boy reached out his hands, wrists together. "Sometimes I wonder what took you so long."

Aaren kneeled in mild disbelief. The punishment for stealing a bag of produce from a store was one year imprisonment, regardless of age. One year away from his brothers, who relied on him for survival. One year in a cell at a time when he should be in school or playing with friends. One year to pay for the equivalent of a couple meals for Aaren.

Even if the boy knew anything about the Cotters, Aaren knew he wasn't going to tell him. *And that's my primary assignment, right?* He stared at the boy, looked at the fence, stood up, and put his dashglass back on.

"Go."

"What?" Now it was the boy who was in disbelief.

"I said go, get on. I can see you'd learn nothing from a year in jail, so why bother feeding you on the public dime— but you should know that any other officer in my place would take you in and not think twice about it. So I hope *you* think twice about stealing next time."

The boy slowly lowered his wrists, his eyes fixed on Aaren, his feet firmly planted. He hesitated.

"Apply for a food grant and use my name as a sponsor." The words came out before Aaren could register what he was saying. *Where did that come from?* "My name is Aaren Jemmer...can you remember that?"

"Hey, my last name is Jemmer too!" The boy eased a bit, genuinely smiling.

Aaren was mildly stunned. It was a common last name, but...

"Yes, I'll remember. Thank you, Officer Jemmer!" The boy took off in a fit of energy, not waiting for Aaren to change his mind.

Aaren waited until the boy disappeared from view before turning to make his way back to the store. A boy who might have been him.

_____

LATE MORNING, EPSILON RING

Her eyes open to a man and a woman, both in surgical masks and white gowns, talking to each other above her. She tries to move her hands but feels them bound. She tries to move her lips but feels them wrapped around a tube—and paranoia spreads down her spine as she groans. Immediately, the man and the woman standing above her look down and begin shouting, and the man reaches for something out of her field of vision...

Natasha woke up with a start, her head jumping off the desk on which it had fallen, her hands thrown up into the air. It was a nightmare she had had many times before, but one she never understood. She closed her eyes and willed her heartbeat down to a normal pace, and with the back of her left hand patted the sweat off her temples. Calming, she looked up at the screen in front of which she'd spent the last several hours in the data room. All of a sudden the room was a bit too warm, and she took off her jacket.

She refocused on her research with heavy eyelids, but not ten minutes later her hand absentmindedly reached for her flask of water and she missed, knocking it to the floor.

Natasha snapped awake to pick it up, relieved that she'd capped it after her last sip. Still, it was a sign; she needed to rest, and so she got up to leave for her bed.

Pausing to stretch, Natasha reflected on her long night turned morning, an exhaustive search of the president's history for something personal and deeply compromising. Something to discredit him, damage his support, and cost him his eighty-percent-of-the-electorate goal. There were public records of his previous terms, his campaign during the first Election, but before that…nothing. No information on him during the wars, on his childhood and upbringing, on anything. Well, nothing public or in the government databases she was able to hack into, anyway. She sighed.

As she made her way to her quarters, one thought kept coming back to her: she needed someone in Alpha or Beta who had access to more confidential information—or someone who could at least point her in the right direction. But who? With just over two days left, who was she going to find? She was out of time—and there was always plan B. There had always been plan B. Assassination.

If she had one shot and it needed to be fatal, maybe it needed to be done literally? But she couldn't do that. And frankly it just couldn't be done; the Resistance had proven that, had they not? When she began her original campaign with the Cotters, she'd sworn a nonviolent approach and thus far had not been able to bring herself to fire a single bullet (Adler, on the other hand, more than made up for it).

Violence had raged for thousands of years, and where had it gotten them? Besides, propaganda pierced sharper than a bullet. *I need someone on the inside…* She barely finished the thought before passing out on her Haline-standard camper's cot.

Just a few hours later she woke, panting, sweaty. A single thought filled her completely: she was out of time. Natasha got up and made her way to the office to find Adler studying a holomap of the city with several others working at their stations.

"Do you think we could get close enough…to…to kill him?" The room went quiet. "I know it goes against everyth…" Her voice drifted off. She inhaled sharply to force herself more awake.

"Never mind." *It would make a martyr out of him and make the government only stronger. Vice President Martin would be worse.*

Adler and the others in the room stared in mild shock at their leader, who had from the beginning vehemently chosen influence over assassination.

"I…can get Marie and Becker briefed and—"

"No, forget I said it. I'm on so little sleep that I'm becoming delusional. I'm heading back to bed, but I want a list of everyone we have with possible access to restricted files. Go back a generation…anyone mildly sympathetic. Let's see if we can find someone who knows something we don't. Have a full report ready by 1600 hours."

"Yes, ma'am. We'll have it ready. We started putting something like that together just a couple days ago."

"All right...come wake me at ten till, 'kay?"

"Get some rest, Natasha."

Natasha walked out the door, but turned right around and walked back in. "Show me what you've already got. Let's just do this now."

There was a pause around the room. The Cotters had been losing support year after year as the status quo became more and more accepted as the status quo. Most of her once-vast team had left, and though many that stayed were almost religious about the movement and what it stood for, the sacrifices eventually wore on them too. A few of her most committed staff had even asked to sit this Election out. It was moments like this, though, that those who remained remembered *why* they remained—and why they continued to trust Natasha despite their failing efforts and waning support.

The troops sprang into action. Adler got up and moved to the screen while Gini and Ronick headed to the data room for more research.

"The reason we halted this search is because everyone seemed compromised."

"Show me the list." Natasha stood up straight and inhaled sharply again, this time to gain focus. Her meditation training was one of her greatest assets.

"Bringing it up now. Eyn, show us the results of search

query 'Insiders,'" Adler said to the screen.

"Stand by, Adler." The government may have had SAI, but the Cotters had Eyn. Not as ubiquitous but damn fast and, most importantly, completely off the grid.

"Eyn, filter out anyone deceased; I don't need to be any more depressed seeing old friends." Adler turned to Natasha, "Trust me, you won't want to see those names either."

Natasha offered a slight nod in reply, then added, "Eyn, show us the children of each result as well." Turning to Adler, "We should be able to tell by the parents something about their upbringing and if they'll have a sympathetic ear or not."

Adler nodded. "All right, here we go—first result, Barron Phills...Department of Commerce, that's interesting. Parents...ha, no, no way. Next result, Eyn. Okay, Lauren Reeve...Department of Intelligence, yeah, no. Next result, Eyn. Santi Cann, Congress...nope. Next. Nope, not her either, next. No, next. Next. Next. Next. Next. Next."

"End of active results that fit search criteria," Eyn replied.

Natasha dropped her head in defeat and exhaustion as Adler's team emerged back into the room. Another sharp breath. *Focus. Head up.* "Find anything guys?"

"Not much." Gini had a confused look on her face. "We were able to come up with one more name. Eyn missed it as the last name is different than the parents' but we stitched it together manually by cross-referencing official records against our own unofficial register. His classification seems impossible, but we're pretty sure he is the offspring. It just doesn't make any sense."

"Who are the parents?"

"Alyel and Soel Nosa."

"I remember them...strong supporters and early donors. Doctors at Central Hospital if I recall. Eyn, bring it up on screen." Natasha paused as a face flashed up.

"Wait, that can't be right." Natasha turned to Gini. "How could they have birthed an officer?"

The face had a name: Lieutenant Aaren Jemmer.

4

"Am I really a descendent of the Jemmer family? Let me ask you this: does it matter anymore? The continuing legacy of generosity and support of the family name is, I believe, what matters most. If my grandparents were self-anointed Jemmers who forged documents for the safety of their family, so long as they honored the name once accepted into the tribe, to me I am a true descendent. Who wouldn't, if they could, change their last name to belong to a people who provided and protected their own?"

— President Gaven Jemmer, semiannual press briefing,
first year in office

SAME DAY
LATE AFTERNOON, BETA RING

It was almost 1600 hours and most of the office had cleared out, but the diligent Joaquin Deva had a few more things left to do before his holiday began. As deputy librarian at the Archives Department, Joaquin evaluated confiscated materials. Sometimes they came in from raids of suspected Resistance, Cotter, or enemy establishments, other times from routine demolition of prewar and wartime homes. Joaquin's job was simply to determine what was to be preserved and what incinerated.

Deciding which was which was easy—anything that supported the Haline government or that chronicled the struggle of the wars was to be archived; everything else, destroyed.

At times it frustrated Joaquin that his superiors mandated he dispose of so many utterly harmless yet fascinating artifacts. Once, a multicolored puzzle cube crossed his desk that had him mesmerized for hours. Another time, a hook-and-line device that, after some research, he learned was used to catch fish—*just catch them!*—before they had largely disappeared from lakes and rivers and streams.

It was an interesting job that Joaquin was lucky to get that allowed him to see and touch and learn about a not-so-distant past forgotten by most. After studying history at university at his uncle's suggestion—"in order to understand the present, and from there the future"—it was the best he could have hoped for.

Joaquin's mind floated back to one of his last conversations with his uncle just a few weeks before he died four years earlier.

"Tell me again, Joaquin."

"Uncle...what does it matter? That world is gone."

"It matters because it is the 'why' to answer the question 'why are we here.' Few fathers or mothers or uncles care to remember the why, but your parents would have wanted you to know, and I want you to know. Now tell me again."

Joaquin sat in a chair next to his uncle's bed holding his hand. They both knew there wasn't much more time, that they wouldn't be seeing each other like this for much longer. Joaquin squeezed his uncle's hand, stood up, and began pacing while sharing what his uncle had drilled into him in his youth.

"Well, Uncle, as you know history books describe the world before the wars as greedy, self-interested, and blindly proud. Somewhere along the line these attitudes, combined with incredible advances in technology, led to careless exploitation of natural resources that caused such pollution that it artificially warmed the planet. This triggered a chain of events that led to a shutdown of the thermohaline flow, which in turn...Uncle?"

"Yes, yes, Joaquin, I'm here...just closing my eyes and remembering those days. Continue please. Slower though...visualize the world you are describing. Stand there in it and see it...breath in the acrid pollution, smell the burn in the air, taste the rotting fields of produce."

"Yes, Uncle." Joaquin stopped pacing, took a deep breath, and closed his eyes to imagine. "The shutdown of the thermohaline flow..."

Joaquin saw the complex movement of water through the oceans choking to a halt, one result of the excessive accumulation of carbon dioxide in the atmosphere that had passed a tipping point. He saw millions of fish and sharks and whales and dolphins turn belly up and float to the water's surface in mass watery graves.

"...led to unfettered species extinction worldwide as

temperatures fluctuated and food chains broke down. The resulting biospheric disruption, together with the schizophrenic weather post-flow, caused extensive crop failures and massive losses of livestock..."

Joaquin pictured the endless fields of dying crops and inhaled the putrid stench of rotting chicken and pig and cattle at farm after farm after farm. He felt nauseated.

"Which led to poverty and famine, which in turn led to mass migrations and a massive uptick in the spread of disease. This was followed by global territory and resource wars that lasted over two decades."

Joaquin paused to feel the immense gravity of every word he was about to utter, and his nausea shifted to a dizziness. He sat to keep the room still.

"When all was said and done, Uncle, only about 850 million of the world's prewar and pre-famine population survived."

"That's right, Joaquin, less than one in ten of the nine billion that used to walk our planet's surface. Think about that and you'll understand why no one wants to remember— and why we must remember." His uncle opened his eyes and looked at him with a grave seriousness that Joaquin was surprised to see in his frail frame.

"Come, get me my medicine." Coming out of his trance, his uncle sat up. "You know, we didn't have to swallow these damn anti-microalgae spore pills when I was a kid, Joaquin. The air we had evolved with over billions of years used to

come in and out of our lungs in perfect balance—not
saturated with disease-causing spores. And where did the
spores come from? Us! Bioengineered to absorb carbon from
the atmosphere, we blindly released them into the oceans
not thinking through the implications."

His uncle paused to look at the pills in his palm. "To me,
they are a daily reminder of everything we lost."

Joaquin's attention came back to his emptied-out
office. Shaking his head, he remembered Lyla would be
expecting him home soon. His eyes turned to the few items
that remained on his desk for processing.

A small datacard of prewar design piqued his interest.
He saw on the screen it had been uncovered at the old
presidential bunker, which was undergoing renovation for
occupancy by the vice president. Joaquin picked it up and
walked it over to ISA, the department's Independent Security
Archive mainframe. Someone important had decided long
ago that ISA should be independent from SAI in case she
were ever compromised. Joaquin activated the card.

ISA got to work and immediately identified several
thousand frames and vids on the card. The screen began
flashing through them, one by one. The first was a vacation,
by the looks of it. Some place by the ocean with rocky cliffs.
ISA ran simultaneous facial recognition, identifying any
people in each frame. Sitting back in his chair, Joaquin
stretched...this could take several minutes. But then he had
only two more items to process and he'd be done and out

the door for four days to spend with Lyla.

He cringed in self-embarrassment that a part of him wished he didn't have the time off. Not that he didn't enjoy spending his free time with Lyla...just that he didn't know if he *wanted* to spend his free time with her—or anyone. As they grew closer together and walked down the path toward marriage, he found himself conflicted about almost everything in his life and what he wanted from it. *But I love her...right?*

"Give me audio on the names." Joaquin got up to get some coffee from the back of the office as ISA began announcing names of identified people. "Jules L. Frommer, Unidentifiable, Darius J. Levdon, Rebi A. Tomland."

He poured a short cup and mixed in his allowed single portion of cream and double portion of sugar. "Benoit A. Tisch, Rahman J. Sipton, Unidentifiable."

The coffee felt good against the back of his throat, and Joaquin closed his eyes to savor the warmth. "Aby G. Robey, Henri L. Robey." The texture. The aroma. The taste. "Gaven B. Jemmer."

The coffee nearly fell from his hands. Joaquin whipped around with a "Hold search!" and moved quickly to the screen. *It couldn't be the same one.* Oh, but the resemblance..."ISA, magnify."

It was him...it must be him. A young President Jemmer stood smiling with his arm around someone, the ocean magnificent behind them. "ISA, who's the other person in this frame?"

"Unidentifiable."

Joaquin peered in closer. He knew that face but...from where? Joaquin felt SAI's ears in the room even though he had been promised she had no presence there. "Resume search, ISA. And cut audio."

His eyes were glued to the screen now, and after several more frames of President Jemmer at the ocean, the images moved to what seemed to be the front lines of a war. The growing persons list next to the frames contained names that sounded more and more familiar, just as the images started looking more and more foreign. *Is that the president with a gun to someone's head?*

"Hold search." He was barely a hundredth of the way through the card, but he'd seen more than enough. Joaquin slowly sat down in his chair and stared blankly at the screen in front of him.

There was no reason why today should be different from any other day for Joaquin. He should destroy the datacard, archive or destroy the two items remaining on his desk, log out, and head home to have dinner with Lyla— perhaps stopping by the store for the fresh groceries she'd probably have ordered.

And yet.

His mind raced at the implications of the frames he'd seen and what more could be on the card. In his two years in the department he'd encountered the occasional contraband he knew was somehow more dangerous than he should have been allowed to see (the director always took an initial pass at anything that came in), but after satisfying his curiosity he incinerated the potentially offending artifact—always considering the implications of doing so but doing so nonetheless. Occasionally, he would take home an item for his collection, but it would always be something he felt was fairly innocuous, like his new old watch. Joaquin always did what his uncle taught him to do: the right thing.

But this...this was different. Far from a harmless bygone, this was...severe. And at a level he could only begin to fathom.

It's a test. They're monitoring my reaction to the images. For the first time in as long as he could remember, Joaquin felt the beat of his heart. It was faster than he remembered being normal. *No, not today, just days before an Election. Okay, it's a fabrication. But what if it's not? I need more time. I need—*

His transceiver rang and he jumped. SAI told him it was Lyla. He inhaled sharply and closed his eyes, moving his fingers to the bridge of his nose, where he squeezed as he exhaled to release the stress. Then he answered, "Hey, babe."

"Hey, you almost done? I'll bet you're the only person at the office. Everyone I know is already on their way to Zeta for the holiday."

"Lyla, you said—"

"It's fine, I'm not saying we should go. Can you come home though, please? And swing by the store on your way? I patched in an order."

"I need another twenty minutes but will try to hurry. See you soon?" He hoped she didn't sense the tension in his voice.

"Fine, yes, byyyye."

"Bye."

Joaquin muted his transceiver and sat motionless. He again reminded himself what he should do, lest he'd forgotten: get up, log out, T-bus to get groceries, and T-bus home. With that, he got up, ejected the datacard, slipped it into a restricted book he pulled off the shelf, logged out, left the office, T-bussed to get the groceries, and skipped the T-bus from there to walk the rest of the way home. Safer.

―――――――――――
LATE AFTERNOON, BETA RING

Lieutenant Aaren Jemmer sat at his workstation checking reports from his field team as they secured and closed key government buildings in advance of the Election. The "holiday," a strategy architected by the president to allow the police to lock down critical parts of Haline in the days leading up to and just after the Election. *Brilliant.*

Aaren despised being in the office sitting at his workstation, but another fifteen minutes and he'd be back in the field resuming his search for the Cotters. He'd received high praise for their recent lack of activity, ever since he was assigned responsibility to monitor and block any potential Cotter activity in advance of the Election. The relative calm boded well for his upcoming performance review, but he was not quite sure he deserved the credit. Frankly, his job had been relatively easy, and he'd made remarkably little progress.

Leaning back in his chair, his mind went back to the first Election when that wasn't the case. Fresh out of the Academy at the top of his class, he'd expected preferred placement—but to be assigned to the elite Military Police Force that implemented and enforced the Transition was unexpected; he wasn't sure whether it was an honor or some kind of punishment. He smiled remembering his worst fears: *they know!*

In those days just after the wars, dispersed patches of Resistance fighters not willing to accept the new government made for a violent peace. Of course, Aaren was a lot more afraid back then. More anxious to prove himself. More ready to shed blood in the name of Haline. His mind went to the first time he killed a man. A young, young man...

Aaren crouches outside the fortified complex waiting for the order to proceed with the offensive. Inside, members of the Resistance prepare to defend their commandeered coal-fired power plant, refusing to participate in the transition to solar. He hears their yells as they scramble to regroup, and in a moment of disbelief Aaren realizes the only reason he is here is to silence those voices, forever.

He instinctively turns his head to see the remnants of the outer gate that his team had just blasted through and remembers the chief's words: "Our move off of fossil fuel will not be easy. Yes, the wars have fractured production, and many have already made the transition to solar to eliminate dependence on the grid, but energy is power—and right now, all that people are fighting and dying for is power."

"Green!" Before the order is finished Aaren is on his feet in full sprint, shots coming at him from ahead, shots being returned from behind. He reaches one of the doors to an office-type building, places a charge on it, and runs along the side of the complex to avoid the explosion.

Nestled in a crevice he waits for the smoke to clear, counts to ten while listening for gunfire, then pushes off of his back to move in—coming face to face with a teenager rushing out. There is a gun in each of their hands, but neither seems to know it as they stand there eyes wide, breath short, heart fast.

The teenager moves his gun hand, and before he knows he's doing it, Aaren fires. Impossibly, the teenager's eyes widen even more as the gun drops from his hand and he falls forward onto Aaren.

"I was...I..." the teenager goes limp in Aaren's arms as Aaren slowly lowers him to the ground. Standing above him, Aaren looks into the once-full eyes as they become vacant. Gripped by an emotion he struggles to hide, Aaren refuses to

believe the first thought in his head and the accompanying feeling that attacks his chest: the boy was moving to drop his gun, not aim it. No! *The boy was moving to drop his gun, not aim it.* No! No! No! No! No!

A blinking red light on one of his screens brought him back: a datacard had been removed from the Archives by a Gamma-class, G2-security-clearance government employee. Normally, not a cause for concern, but this close to the Election..."SAI, add address of offender to Gamma sweep for this evening."

It'd give him something to do before going home to an empty apartment.

_____

LATE AFTERNOON, GAMMA RING

Natasha was confused. She'd run the search two more times to make sure she was reading the results correctly. "Gini, are you certain the records irrefutably have his parents as Alyel and Soel?"

"Yes, Natasha. We ran the search and cross-referenced the result three times before bringing it to you. We didn't believe it ourselves."

"Alyel and Soel..."

"They were early in joining the Cotter movement, but they died in the Massacre." Gini was looking down at a screen, reading Alyel's bio.

"Looks like Aaren was born just over a month before.

They must have feared or even known the boycott would turn violent." Adler peered at his screen skimming over Aaren's public record.

"Fine, so they wanted to protect their son. But an officer?" Gini looked up with anger in her eyes. Her parents had been jailed and tortured for protesting against the genetic engineering of officers.

"He probably doesn't know who his parents are..." Natasha stared into a distance.

"He can't know. He's an officer!" Gini put the screen down harder than she intended and inhaled to regain her calm.

"He must think he's been genetically enhanced like his peers. Or maybe, he's realized he's not. Actually, he's surely realized that by now." Adler looked up from his screen.

"Yeah, and he's probably had a hard time of it too, originally thinking he shared their strengths." Natasha's voice was matter of fact. "Even if he's anywhere near as tall, there's no way he is as fast or as strong. You're right, he must know he's not one of them..."

Her voice slowed down as her thoughts sped up. "Say you're an officer and know you aren't supposed to be. What would you do?"

Adler looked down to picture it. "Fake it. Work harder than everyone else so no one finds out. What other option does he have?"

"None. But he knows he doesn't belong. That he's not

one of them. And now we know. And if he's still an officer, we're probably the only ones to know he's a fraud." She paused. "No one likes to feel like a fraud."

They turned to each other with a shared look of hope and fear and held it a moment. Were they really going to actively seek out a lieutenant in the Haline Police and expose themselves as Cotters?

"Let's find him." Natasha's voice was firm.

_____

LATE AFTERNOON, BUNKER ONE, CITY CENTER

The president sat in his office and glanced up from the screen on his desk to the screen on the wall, which displayed the latest poll estimates. A satisfied grin splashed across his face as his chest protruded with confidence and his fingers drummed a beat. A member of his Citizen Guard knocked, opened the door, and reminded him—two minutes until he was scheduled for dinner with the vice president. The guard left, closing the door behind him.

He was just about to get up when his desk beeped twice, softly. He froze and quickly glanced up at where his CG soldier had stood just a few seconds prior. They knew he was alone, but the beeps always made the president jump and make sure no one was listening. Swiping his thumb, he simultaneously locked the door to his office and unlocked the hidden side drawer in his grand desk.

The screen lifted into place and tilted in his direction

with a message—a frame of him and another at the ocean many years ago, before the wars, and below it some text:

> *A pre-Haline datacard was lost in the move from your old bunker. Yesterday it was discovered and submitted to Archives, including this frame and hundreds more compromising. Gamma-class employee Joaquin Deva, G2 security clearance, processed the card this evening. Instead of incinerating it, he removed it from Archives. Find it and destroy it immediately.*

Sweat broke out on the president's brow and his heart rate doubled as he read the note a second time. His mouth gaped without a word.

The guard tried the door and, finding it locked, knocked loudly. "Sir, every—"

The president's head snapped up. "Gimme one goddamn minute, will you!"

5

"Today, one hundred percent of our energy comes from sun and wind sources that we harvest without corporate exploitation and lies. If our ancestors had seen the sad truths of their times they might have prevented thermohaline shutdown, but they did not. So we have shut down these corporations and abandoned their disastrous methods to prevent future wars so our children may live better lives than ours."

— President Gaven Jemmer's State of the Union,
second term, first year

THREE DAYS UNTIL ELECTION
EARLY EVENING, GAMMA RING

Joaquin walked in, put the canvas bag of groceries on the table, and moved to give Lyla a quick kiss.

"You were the last one there, weren't you."

"Lyla, you know how I am about work, especially before a vacation. But look, now we have four days off! What are we going to do?"

"Well, I see you picked up something to read."

Joaquin missed having pockets. After the first Election it was decreed that pockets could hide nefarious and contraband items, and so they were disallowed. It was a small book that could have easily been tucked away in his old jacket; now he prayed she didn't ask to see it.

"Yeah, well...you know me. I'm going to change for

dinner and try to think of something fun for us to do. Do the same and let's compare notes?"

Joaquin jumped up the stairs to the bedroom two steps at a time, turned to make sure she hadn't followed (*why would she follow?*) and put the book on a shelf of brothers and sisters where it hid in plain sight. For once, he was thankful Lyla didn't like to read much. After a quick body wipe—he had already taken his allowed three-minute shower in the morning—Joaquin changed and was about to head back down when the watch caught his eye. Grabbing it off the counter, his fingers fumbled trying to fasten it while casually bobbing down each step, proudly appreciating the completed work on his wrist when he got to the bottom of the stairs. Back in the kitchen, where Lyla was setting the table, he reached for the wine glasses in the cabinet.

"The congressional leader's daughter. Cooking, cleaning, setting. You should be ashamed." Her voice was flat, making it tough for Joaquin to tell if she was joking.

"C'mon, babe, let's not forget who picked up who at that bar in Beta. You wanted to see what Gamma nightlife was like, remember?"

A tenuous smile flashed across Lyla's face before she forced a frown. "Maybe I made a mistake."

Joaquin put the wine glasses down on the table, walked up behind where she was plating dinner on the counter, and kissed the back of her neck—slowly and with intention.

"Joaquin! Dinner is ready."

"So am I."

"Well, dinner first. And take that ugly thing off your wrist."

"No." He smiled. "And fine, if that's what you prefer. I have my list…three ideas for us. You?"

They sat down to dinner and began discussing options: Zeta Ring, a movie marathon, shopping, errands, visiting with friends (whoever was left in town), reading (Lyla didn't like this one). Then Lyla suggested something that caught Joaquin off guard.

"What if we went to the Ministry in Beta and brushed up on our history?"

Joaquin looked up, quelling the anger that softly blossomed like a poisonous flower inside him. She must have known this would set him off. She was looking for a fight. He willed himself to a simmering calm.

"Lyla, with all due respect to your father and his storied sacrifices during the wars, you know that I, more than most, am aware that the 'history' as told by the Ministry is a crock of shit, pardon my language. And I, more than most, definitely do *not* need any brushing up."

"Just because you get glimpses of knickknacks—"

"*Knickknacks?* History is my passion, you know—"

"That doesn't mean you *understand* history. My mother says—"

"So this is about your mother."

Lyla's face hardened. "What does that mean?"

"It's just that you're overprotective of her because she's part of the same Congress that—"

Her faced tightened as she stood up from her chair. "Don't you ever, ever disrespect my mother. She's done more for Haline than—"

"I'm not disrespecting. On the contrary—"

"Shut up! I'm not ashamed that my mother is part of the government!"

"I didn't say you should be!"

Lyla started sobbing. Being the daughter of a historically notable pre-Haline hero was burdensome—but being the current congressional leader's daughter was downright arduous. In the early days when policies that provided more access to water or food were passed, she was a celebrity among friends and foes alike.

But as time went on and a rift formed between the president and Congress, most sided with the president as they believed him their one true savior. Congressional Leader Danyela Clarek was the rare figure who fervently stood up to the president's growing power, but through the filter of the executive branch-controlled HN, Danyela Clarek's people-minded efforts were distorted.

Calming, Lyla lowered her head and whispered. "My dream...it's been bothering me. I'm worried about her—" before startling as she remembered SAI was listening. *Maybe dreams* are *illegal.*

She lifted her head and looked squarely at Joaquin with

a face expressing equal parts fear and love, neither directed at him. "I should go. I haven't visited mother in almost a week and she'll be happy to see me. Especially with the Election in a few days."

Joaquin was ashamed that the emotion that now swelled inside of him was relief, and he desperately tried to match her anguish. "I understand…"

He rose from the table to comfort her. "Want to plan on hanging out the day after tomorrow?" As the words left his mouth, he thought of the datacard and realized they might only ever be words. *Am I lying?*

"Yeah…sounds good." Joaquin and Lyla embraced for a long moment. For her part, Lyla held Joaquin for his unwavering support of her and her mother, perhaps the only person in the world who she believed would steadfastly stand by them no matter the consequences.

For his part, Joaquin held Lyla because a growing part of him believed it might be a while before he would hold her again. While he wasn't sure what secrets the card kept, he had a gnawing sense of their magnitude and the strong feeling that he wouldn't be able to contain his desire to uncover those secrets, no matter the cost. His arms squeezed tighter and he wondered again if what he felt for Lyla was called love. *This is probably it.*

Lyla left, and the door slid shut behind her. Joaquin leaned back on it while he paused to think a moment. He walked upstairs one slow step at a time, opened the book, and held the datacard in his hand where he stood, frozen in thought—debating, pondering, worrying, deciding, dithering, changing his mind, and deciding again.

For all his adult life he'd relished the study of history, working to understand what was and what had been, piecing together a picture of the prewar world that had existed for millennia. This datacard perhaps had some of the answers he sought, but there was no one he could show its contents to. The only person in the world he trusted, his uncle, was gone.

He stared at his bookshelf, moving from title to title. He'd read them all. He'd read everything he could get his hands on. But nothing he'd learned explained the images he'd seen, and slowly Joaquin realized that the first idea that came to mind—which he dismissed as quickly as it occurred to him—was the only idea he had: the Cotters.

If there was anyone who could help him unlock and understand the contents of the datacard in his hand, it was them. *If uncle had had the health, he surely would have been one of them, right? How bad can they be?*

Joaquin sat and closed his eyes, the card still in his hand. He inhaled clarity, held a breath of insight, exhaled an answer: *If he were me, Uncle would take the card to the Cotters.* Joaquin put the card back in the book, packed a bag, grabbed his jacket, and was out the door less than twenty minutes after Lyla—but before hitting the road he knocked on his neighbor's door. Someone should know where he was going in case something went wrong.

"Hey, am I interrupting anything?" he offered as the door slid open.

"Think I'd answer the door if you were?" Han flashed Joaquin a spry smile.

"Well, you always answer the door, so I thought to ask." Joaquin smiled back. He wondered if this might be the last time he saw Han for a while but fought the thought away. *I'll be back in a day or two.*

"Listen, can you watch the place? I'm heading out for the night."

Joaquin knew he could trust Han but didn't want to tell him too much—for his own sake. So, just the basics: Lyla was going to her mother's and he was going to head out to the border between Gamma and Delta to read a book off the restricted list in peace. This one was *highly* restricted, so he wanted to be sure no one stumbled upon him reading it, and he sure wasn't spending his vacation alone in his apartment.

"Yeah, I get it. You'd prefer some boring story by a dead guy over hanging out with your best friend. Whatever."

"You sound surprised."

"Get out of here. Just make sure you don't get killed by the Resistance. Or caught by a Cotter. I hear those crazies hang out in droves in the borders."

Good old Han. I knew I could count on you. Joaquin gave Han a knowing glance and replied. "Do they?"

Before Han could understand what he was getting at Joaquin was down the stairs. He didn't get far before his transceiver rang...it was Han.

"Hey, umm...you sure about this? Sleeping in the border area might not be the smartest...with all the mosquitoes out. It's a warm night."

Joaquin read between the lines. "I'll be fine. This is something I need to do."

"All right, Joaquin. Be safe. I'll be waiting to hear from you. Call me tomorrow morning, okay?"

"I'll message as soon as I'm back in range." Citizen transceiver signals were disabled in border regions to make them dead zones between Rings. They'd thought of everything.

**

Aaren pressed the buzzer and waited just a few seconds before asking SAI if anyone was home. "Joaquin Deva is not home. He left twenty-four minutes ago and is on a T-bus heading toward Delta Ring."

Not terribly surprising; it is, after all, the start of a vacation. A bit late but..."SAI, Lieutenant Aaren Jemmer requesting access to the unit."

In these more quiet days, it made Aaren a bit uneasy having access to any apartment or home he wanted to enter. It was a power that had been abused by many an officer, so he used it sparingly—but this was one of those times. "Access granted." The door unlocked and slid open.

The unit was nothing special...standard issue for Gamma-class government employees. A reclaimed complex from before the wars, it had been retrofitted for water and energy conservation, standard appliances, and finished off with the requisite monitoring and surveillance systems. It took Aaren just a few minutes to thoroughly cover the one-bedroom apartment. Nothing out of the ordinary, but a large—had he ever seen one larger?—book collection. A few overdue books from the restricted list sat on a table next to the crowded shelf, but not the one he was looking for and no sign of the datacard.

On went his dashglass. "SAI, play apartment vids five-minutes prior to exit." His frame split into four for the four cameras placed around the unit. Nothing out of the ordinary, but Joaquin did grab the book in question and stood with it in his right hand for a curiously long time, and seemed to be holding something in his left hand—likely the card.

"SAI, show me door cam." A visit to the neighbor…just a few minutes. Maybe he told him where he was heading? "Hold frame, SAI."

**

When he saw it was an officer on the door-view screen, Han hesitated for a second but quickly regained composure and calmly pushed the button to open the door. It unlocked and slid along its glide rail—*pshhhhhht.*

"Hey, Officer, what can I do for ya?"

"Citizen Remi, did Joaquin tell you where he was going?"

Han wasn't surprised the officer got straight to the

point with full knowledge that Joaquin had left for the night with no need to explain the situation. Officers had access to SAI and SAI knew everything, so citizens, therefore, expected officers to know everything.

"Not specifically. Just that he was heading out for a day or two. We're quite close…he knew I'd miss him."

Aaren wanted to give Han a glaring look, but Han's casual demeanor was disarming.

"Thank you, citizen. Enjoy your vacation. And don't forget to vote."

"I won't, Officer. Forget, that is." Han gave Aaren a smile that Aaren held for a curious moment before turning to walk down the stairs.

The door slid shut and Han went straight for his transceiver to call Joaquin, but Joaquin's transceiver was off; he must have already arrived at the border. No way to ask him why an officer was looking for him. Or to warn him.

**

Shortly before the second Election, in supposed response to citizen complaints that the police had too much power and were not only anywhere but everywhere, the government made public the whereabouts of on-duty officers on regular patrols. This gave citizens some peace. If they were going to commit a minor infraction—say, break curfew—they at least had a chance at avoiding getting caught. Of course, more than half the police force were incognitos—or "incogs" as they were called—and SAI knew everything all the time anyway. Still, it was a small win that pacified the people.

Lucky for Natasha, Lieutenant Aaren Jemmer must have been on duty and conducting regular patrols, as his location was being broadcast. He was in the Gamma Ring, apparently on a sweep of government housing there.

"Now's our chance. Once he finishes his patrol he'll head home to Beta Ring, where we can't follow," Gini turned from her screen to Natasha.

"Yup, let's move. Adler, stay here and keep hacking. See if you can figure out a way for a mass broadcast burst, even one that exposes our location or requires us to be at Central Station in Alpha. At this point, the craziest ideas are the only ones we have yet to try. Gini, Ronick, you're with me."

"Natasha, Aaren just dropped off the grid. He's in sector 4G on an apartment visit—but went dark." Gini's face melted.

"It's too early for him to be off duty...he must have found something. Adler, patch me the address. Maybe he's still in the neighborhood. Let's *go*!"

Natasha, Gini, and Ronick surfaced and hastily made their way to the T-sub station, swiped their reprogrammed wrists above the turnstiles, and boarded the open cabin. Natasha pulled her hat close down over her face and wore a citizen-class dashglass that modified her iris pattern for SAI's eyeball scanners.

Less than fifteen minutes later they were in sector 4G,

and Natasha, Gini, and Ronick moved off the train and waded through the crowd, watchful for any officers. Within minutes, they surfaced from the station onto the street and walked briskly toward Aaren's last known location. Gini and Ronick waited downstairs while Natasha bounded up the stairs two at a time, quickly composed herself with a deep breath, and buzzed.

A brownish-skinned man opened the slide door, a look of confusion-meets-pleasant-surprise across his face. "Yeess?"

"Hey, sorry to bother. There was an officer here a bit ago who I'm trying to track down. Long story, I...owe him a debt." Natasha smiled, an embarrassed look on her face. Officers would often overlook minor infractions in return for various contraband—or favors. Though she kept her hair closely cropped unlike the style of the day, Natasha exuded a glowing beauty about her. He'd believe it.

"Oh." The look of surprise gave way to disappointment. "Yeah, he came by looking for my buddy—not that my buddy did anything wrong, mind you—but left. Didn't tell me where he was going."

"Okay. Hmm...do you know where your buddy was going?"

"Uh...out?" A flash of suspicion crept into Han's eyes. "Why do you ask?"

Natasha hesitated, trying to think of another question. She needed more information. Was he nice? Did he seem like a real officer or more like one of us? But nothing she could ask would fit the story she'd just given.

"Just trying to find the officer. Sorry to bother...and thanks!" Natasha turned to go.

Han's suspicion morphed back into interest. "Hey uh...I was just opening up a bottle of Alpha-class wine and about to start a movie. You know we're code orange for a tornado tonight, right? You're welcome to sit it out here, if you'd like."

She turned to catch his flirtatious smile and blushed. It'd been a while since anyone had made a pass at her. It was out of the question for anyone on her team, and she rarely interacted with anyone else for fear of being recognized—or distracted.

"Thanks but...I have to go. Some other time." She smiled, genuinely. The first part was honest. Maybe the second part was too. Her heart gave a soft flutter as she turned.

She walked down the stairs to rejoin Gini and Ronick, and her smile fell off to be replaced by her usual look of focus, determination, and resolve. "He's gone. No lead. Let's go."

As the T-sub moved them homeward, Natasha slowly gave up on finding Aaren. With the Election this close he might not pop back on grid for a regular patrol. And besides, the odds were slim he would have cooperated anyway. Back to the drawing board. Two days.

6

"It is hereby decreed that voting for Elections shall be mandatory so that this fledgling democracy, born out of the ashes of war and famine and disease, has the full legitimacy and support of its people. Anyone eligible to vote who boycotts an Election is subject to a fine, or imprisonment if the fine cannot be paid."

— From the Haline Constitution

TWO DAYS UNTIL ELECTION
EARLY MORNING, GAMMA / DELTA BORDER

Joaquin awoke to the sound of a few scattered birds in the trees above his head. Beautiful. Rare. He lay mesmerized by their song. Most birds had died of hunger after the climate shift wiped out their primary food sources, and many of the heartier species that had survived were exterminated for the diseases they began to carry. He couldn't see them, but by their graceful song he guessed these few were descendants of the former.

He'd reached the border between Gamma and Delta just after dark the night before, taking refuge under a grove of juniper trees. As a dead zone policed by the occasional scout, the border was relatively quiet. No food, no water, and without shelter from night temperatures that often dropped below freezing, border regions were intentionally kept unlivable—but the quiet was still beautiful.

Joaquin applied sun cream to his face, neck, and hands. In the border regions, there were also no protective absorption shield to deflect the bulk of the sun's lethal radiation, which penetrated through the weakened atmosphere. Slowly stretching his stiffened muscles, Joaquin realized the night had taken with it some of his adrenaline and resolve, and he wondered exactly what it was he was trying to do.

He had a good life—an enjoyable and stable job, a loving companion, good friends...so why was he possibly jeopardizing all that? Joaquin closed his eyes and got into a meditative pose, his legs crossed and his back straight. Breathing helped him clear his mind. Focus. Understand.

His thoughts kept taking him to his youth and his conversations with his uncle. His parents had died in the Massacre shortly after he was born, and his uncle raised him as his own, not even bothering to tell him that he'd been adopted until he felt Joaquin was old enough to grasp its meaning—and lack of it. It was his uncle who had suggested he apply for a position in the Archives Department. "You'll learn more about history there than in any of these history books you're always reading," he'd said.

In his two years at Archives, Joaquin had seen much but had only learned one thing: things used to be *very* different. It was as if history had been on a more or less straight-line path of mostly forward human progress, albeit with its dark periods, until the climate changed. At that point history changed direction, spiraling inward and collapsing into itself. Basic survival instinct emerged as the prime motivator governing every action, good or—as was often the case— horribly, shockingly bad. For a time, civilization was lost.

And then, some say miraculously, Haline emerged. To all who survived the wars, the safety of Haline was paradise itself. But the more Joaquin learned, the more he began to wonder if Haline's people were truly in the light, or just in a lighter shade of dark. He wasn't yet sure, but the few frames of the datacard he'd seen reinforced his quiet, growing fear that it was more the latter.

Standing up, he stretched again. With his arms extended and reaching, Joaquin regained some of his resolve. Not his time in college, nor his years getting his PhD, nor any single day at the Archives Department had yielded anything close to the possible gold mine that sat compressed between the pages of the book that sat at his feet. He wasn't risking much if the frames on the datacard had been fabricated. And if they weren't…well, he could still return the card to Archives and incinerate it. No one would notice it had been gone a few days. *SAI doesn't have a presence in the Archives Department, remember?* Or so he hoped.

His plan called for the Cotters to find him rather than the other way around. To do that, he need only find a terminal and report a Cotter sighting. Terminals were found on every other block in the Rings—places where you could pull up holomaps or call T-cabs or shop or vote. Of course, they were also fitted with cameras and sensors, serving both the people *and* their government.

At terminals, citizens could also file police reports, including Cotter sightings. It'd be harder to find one in the border area, but Joaquin was certain there would be a few.

The way he figured, if the Cotters were out there and as much a threat as the government said they were, he need only file a false report of a Cotter sighting in the border region to get their attention; the Cotters would know it to be false and might investigate. Joaquin assumed the police would likely ignore it—a single Cotter sighting rarely mobilized a search team. Most likely they'd send a scout, which wouldn't find anything nefarious meriting officer backup. The Cotters would, hopefully, find him.

He rolled his sleeping bag into his backpack, put on his citizen-class dashglass, and walked northeast, careful to stay well clear of the border walls he knew to be a few miles out to both his left and right while he searched for a terminal. It was forty minutes before he found one just outside the edge of a clearing that must have served as a meeting place in months or years past, judging by its artificially oval nature. He took a deep breath—not quite fulfilling, but close—and filed the report. Joaquin took a few steps back contemplating the worst-case-scenario repercussions of his action, then shook his head and sat. It was done. Now it was time to wait.

**

"Joaquin Deva has been identified as still in the border region between Gamma and Delta, sector 7GDB." Aaren was just emerging from his seven-minute shower when his screen changed from the morning news to a map of the border.

Drying his hair, he asked casually, "SAI, how was this information obtained?"

"Citizen Deva filed a report of a Cotter sighting."

Fascinating. On one hand, Joaquin had no idea he was under enhanced surveillance, but on the other, he must know that taking a datacard from Archives would raise an alarm. Or maybe he thought SAI would overlook it, like she overlooked other things he'd taken in the past?

Aaren had seen a lot in his time as an officer, and his mind moved quickly; it was *possible* Joaquin had indeed spotted a Cotter and was reporting it as a good citizen...

"SAI, any cotter movement around there recently? Anything to corroborate Citizen Deva's report?"

"Negative, Lieutenant Jemmer. No cotter activity has been reported in the area for three months, twenty-one days."

I had a feeling you'd say that. It was more likely Citizen Deva was trying to get Cotter attention—perhaps to share the card? If the latter, the missing datacard was now a more serious situation than he had previously thought.

"SAI, notify headquarters I'll investigate." As Aaren ceremoniously snapped on his uniform, he got the rare priority ring on his transceiver. Confused as to who it might be, he answered diplomatically:

"Lieutenant Jemmer here."

"Lieutenant? It's President Jemmer."

Aaren froze. The voice came in thick and loud.

"Listen, I hear you're monitoring a citizen who's stolen a datacard from Archives. This card must not—I repeat, must not—fall into Resistance or Cotter hands. Do I make myself clear?"

Though he'd spoken with the president before, the implications of this personal request caused Aaren to hesitate. "Ye—yes sir. I'll make sure that doesn't happen, sir. Understood, sir."

"Do that. You have authorization to kill him if necessary. In fact, kill him just in case. And make sure that damn datacard does not get accessed by anyone, even you. When you do recover it, patch me in so I can see you destroy it, then bring me back the burned casing. Don't let me down, Aaren. I'm counting on you."

The transceiver line clicked off, and Aaren stood a moment in a fog of shock. He took a deep breath then raced out the door, confused—and for the first time in as long as he could remember, scared.

**

"Natasha, wake up. I think you'll want to see this." Adler turned on the dim lamp that stood by the door and handed his yawning commander a screen. She sat back on her pillow and widened her eyes to force them awake.

"Wait, wasn't Joaquin Deva the citizen Officer Jemmer went to see yesterday?"

"That's right. And there's no way he saw any of us at his current location. None of us are out there. Frankly, no one is ever out there. So I'm thinking…"

"He's trying to find us."

"That's right."

"And if Aaren is looking for him, perhaps he has something we're not supposed to see." Natasha inhaled sharply then exhaled deliberately in an attempt to slow the heart that was beginning to gather speed. "Adler, get me everything we know about Joaquin stat. And suit up for an ETD of five minutes. We're going to find him first."

7

"Why aren't citizens allowed to pass the barricades and gates that protect our outer borders? Because I love them, that's why. Because while we finally have peace within our land, wars still rage without. I will not let a single citizen die for no good reason on my watch, and crossing outside Haline is certain death.

"Our enemies blockade the mountain passes and set fire to our gates, expecting us to cower in fear. But we can and will rise to the challenge if we each play our role, each do our part. Life may not seem easy at times, but is it not easier than it was? Are we not all fed? Life is easier when you don't live in constant fear. We have come far since the wars."

— From President Gaven Jemmer's acceptance speech, second term

---

TWO DAYS UNTIL ELECTION
MORNING, GAMMA / DELTA BORDER

Joaquin walked around the area to get his bearings. The clearing was about one hundred feet in diameter in the shape of a rough oval. On one side, a tangle of dead, beetle-eaten trees stood stoically, dressed by the emerging green of fungus and algae that attempted life from the branches of death. The trees sloped upward and gave way to a vibrant grove of young oaks that stretched back for miles in the direction he had come. *Some great fire must have burned that portion of the dead forest. Making way for rebirth.* Joaquin smiled.

As early morning gave way to midmorning, the sun's heat intensified and forced Joaquin to seek the cover of shade. Realizing there was a nonzero chance that an officer might decide to investigate, Joaquin climbed up the hillside and took refuge among the oaks, finding a spot where he could see and—he hoped—not be seen. He sat and took out the book, figuring it the best way to pass the time. It opened to the datacard. He stared at it, wondering how it had escaped confiscation during the Transition.

"We must let go of our past in order to free our hands and firmly embrace our future," the newly elected President Jemmer had said in those early, turbulent months. Though reluctant, the people were willing to trade in datacards, books, drives, and lives past for the promise of peace and stability in their future—and so history burned. As the incineration teams rolled through the streets, citizens met them with loaded arms hoping that after years of war and suffering the purge could give them a fresh start. There was so much the people wanted to forget.

Where the datacard had come from and how it could contain such dangerous information and be here, with him, he could barely fathom.

Joaquin put the card on the ground, got comfortable against a tree, and opened up to the first page of the book. Not halfway down it, he heard the distant, high-pitched sound of an Alpha-class transport engine. *Do Cotters have access to Alpha-class transports?* Joaquin's brow narrowed as he realized an officer had indeed called his bluff, and his mind froze as the sound approached and seemed to stop forty or so yards away, at the terminal.

Joaquin's body remained calm and his thoughts soon followed. His fear loosened and he moved—slowly—to get a better view of the clearing. It was an officer flanked by two scouts, and Joaquin saw him put on his dashglass.

Joaquin's mind jumped to two options. One, go down and meet the officer—after all, he'd done nothing wrong—and say he thought he'd heard Cotter activity in the night. Surely the officer would thank him and let him be on his way? Or, he could remain hiding, and should the officer discover him he could pretend to be sleeping but offer the same story.

If his plan had worked and the Cotters were on their way, they would be hesitant to try and find him with an officer hanging around—and that's what was important, to make contact with the Cotters. He closed his eyes and made his decision—go and meet the officer and hope that he could be convinced it was a well-intentioned but false alarm.

As Joaquin stood up, two shots rang out followed by the sound of two scout-sized thuds hitting the ground. He froze. Then a loud voice from the clearing reached his ears, and turning his head to the far end of it, he saw her. Though distant, the woman from the datacard frame by the ocean who stood next to President Jemmer emerged into his reality, speaking to the officer: "Aaren, do you know who you are?"

The officer had spun around and raised his weapon squarely at—

"Natasha Biron. Incredible." Though muffled, Joaquin could hear the officer's words. Natasha stopped walking.

"Aaren, turn off your transceiver. Do it now."

"Why should I?"

"I'll turn myself in willingly and have my team of five, all with officer-class minmax guns aimed right at you, stand down. If you don't turn off your transceiver my team will open fire, I'll escape, and your superiors will dishonor your memory by considering you a failure for not complying."

Natasha left Aaren with no choice, and he turned his transceiver off. She began walking slowly again, arms extended, hands open.

"Aaren, listen closely. You're standing there in an officer's uniform, but we both know you weren't born an officer."

Aaren's weapon hesitated, then dropped slightly, then was angrily shaking at Natasha as he took two steps toward her.

"Careful how you speak to an officer, Natasha. How dare you question my genetic privilege." He paused, looking her square in the eyes. "Put down your weapon and lie flat with your face on the ground and your hands behind your back. You're under arrest."

"But that's just the thing, Aaren." Natasha's voice was

calm, pleading. "You weren't born an officer. But at birth you *were* moved into the officer nursery at Central Hospital. It was not what your parents had truly wanted, but it was the only way they believed you'd live a full life in safety, better than they could offer."

"What do you know about my parents!" Aaren took a step toward Natasha and jabbed the gun in the air toward her. "What do you know about anything, Cotter? Get down or I *will* fire. I have authorization to kill you, and if you do not cooperate, I will not hesitate."

Aaren lied. He in fact had explicit orders never to kill Natasha, which he didn't understand—but at this moment he was ready to disobey those orders. A passion he barely knew gripped and disoriented him.

"Aaren, listen to yourself." Natasha slowly lowered to her knees and put down the gun that was holstered around her right thigh and then placed her hands behind her head, her eyes never leaving Aaren's.

"Just look at how angry you are. Officers aren't supposed to get so angry. They're engineered to remain calm in all situations, remember? But look at you. You're emotional."

Aaren stood there, unwavering, not speaking.

"Your father was a doctor in genetics at Central, and your mother a doctor in the emergency room. To give you a better life they smuggled you into the officer nursery. A month later they died in the Massacre." Natasha paused and waited for her words to sink in. "Your parents were Cotters, Aaren."

Aaren took another step forward, then three steps back, not once taking the aim of his gun off of Natasha. He grunted a sound of disdain that was audible even where Joaquin crouched just up the hill. But still the officer said nothing.

"Aaren, we need your help. We are running out of time. If the president gets reelected, it will be the last Election. Deep down you must know this to be true. It's become inevitable. He intends to *abolish Congress*. Think of the consequences! Pushing us—your parent's people, everyone—into further submission will be just the beginning. Thousands of citizens will be imprisoned, perhaps tortured. He has plans, Aaren, dangerous plans—and we can't let him achieve them. You can help us. Only *you* have access."

Joaquin was fixated, a flurry of thoughts going through his head but one simple truth emerging: he must expose himself, *now*. If he waited and the situation deteriorated, he might not get another chance—and if the situation in Alpha was as dire as Natasha made it out to be, if the people of Haline could see some of the frames he'd seen…

"I have what you're both looking for!" Joaquin remained hidden but made sure his voice was heard. Below, he could see them both turn in his general direction, then Aaren quickly turned back to Natasha, who looked confused.

Aaren stared intently at Natasha a moment before

yelling over his left shoulder. "Joaquin, my orders are to kill you on sight. If you surrender I will stay that order and bring you in alive."

And then to Natasha: "You stay out of this. One move and I will put you down." He re-aimed his gun at her chest, and then flipped his transceiver back on.

"SAI, patch me into command." Aaren's eyes remained on Natasha and with each passing second he tried to convince himself that she was lying and that his course of action was clear. But he was failing.

"Aaren, any sign of the suspect?"

"Suspect is in close range, and what's more—I have Natasha. I need support officers and scouts, stat!"

"Yes, sir. Right away."

Joaquin couldn't make out the words, but he knew what had just happened—the officer had called for backup, leaving them only minutes. His mind raced as he contemplated his options...the officer had orders to kill him! Surely with backup on the way the Cotters didn't stand a chance, but perhaps he could get them the datacard before the officers arrived?

Joaquin took a deep breath, stood, and lifted his right leg to step forward. Before he could plant his foot, his arm was yanked behind him and he was forced to fall backward. His impact was cushioned by an embrace and a few words in a sharp whisper: "What the *hell* are you doing?"

Joaquin rolled off and turned to see Han, a look of

exasperated concern on his sweat-lined face. "Han!" he whispered excitedly. "What are you doing here?"

"Making sure you don't get killed." Han stood, grabbed Joaquin's wrist, and pulled him in the direction of the trees away from the clearing—but Joaquin pulled back.

"No! The officer has kill auth on me if I don't turn myself in! Besides, I have something I have to give the Cotters and…this may be my only chance. Before backup arrives and I lose them."

"I don't care what you have! If you head down there right now you're never coming back. Officers are still minutes away, but those Cotters are armed. They don't know who you are or what you have. Whatever it is, we'll figure it out later—but we have to leave *now*." Han's tone was determined, his face stern. Gone was the twinkle of playfulness Joaquin was so accustomed to, and in its place were absolute certainty and resolve.

"But…" Joaquin hesitated, turned to look at the standoff in the clearing, and then turned back to Han. Conflicted, Joaquin accepted his friend's judgment. "All right…let's get out of here."

"Trust me, after what just happened, you won't have any problem finding the Cotters, because they are now looking for *you*." Han and Joaquin disappeared quickly into the forest growth.

Their escape was noisy, and both Natasha and Aaren looked up toward the movement in the trees. On her knees,

Natasha glanced up at Aaren, well aware that in less than a minute he'd be joined by other officers—and she'd be taken into custody. She'd struck a chord, but was it strong enough? For now, it certainly wasn't.

While Aaren's head remained turned in the direction of the hill, Natasha jumped to her feet, and jabbing his wrist, she took his gun. Then with a swift kick of her steel-toed right boot to his left shin and a sweep of his right leg, she took him down and ran.

Aaren spun his head to see her escaping while he fell. He hit the ground then scrambled up in pain and grabbed the backup gun strapped to his left calf, firing repeatedly into the forest after her but unable to see anyone through the trees. Behind him, four officers repelled down from a transport and four scouts hummed in wait of orders.

"You two, that way to Natasha! And you two, that way…to Joaquin! Scouts, follow and report. Do not engage!" Aaren barked his orders and stared blankly in Natasha's direction, fighting to contain his bodily pain in front of his fellow officers, his mind in a state of perfect confusion.

LATE MORNING, BUNKER ONE, CITY CENTER

The president sat at his desk with his head in his hands, his tie loose, and his wits at end. The officer in charge of recovering the datacard had failed and it was unclear where it now was, making it clear to the president that he had a problem the magnitude of which he had yet to face in his presidency. He dreaded what he had to do next, but he had to do it. Gaven Jemmer swiped his finger along the bio-auth strip below his chair to open the hidden drawer in his grand desk and took out the screen to type a message: "The card is still at large. Sending four CG teams and full scout support to track it down and ensure it is destroyed. Should it leak, I already have a press plan to immediately discredit the source."

He sat there, staring at the blinking cursor on the screen. *She was there. She was always there.* The seconds that passed felt like hours.

"You overestimate your influence and underestimate the potential repercussions. If stability is threatened I will take action—and you will suffer. Let's makes sure I don't have to do that."

The president stared at the screen for a few seconds and watched it go blank. Then he got on the phone with his police chief.

8

"Genetic engineering is preserved for our officers because it would be dangerous if available to the public. Could you imagine? Parents choosing hair color, right or left handedness, even skin color...no, like nuclear power from the days before the wars, it's owned by the people and serves the people, but operated by a government that protects the people—sometimes from themselves."

— President Jemmer, Haline Armed Forces open house,
first year in office

_____

TWO DAYS UNTIL ELECTION
AFTERNOON, GAMMA RING

Joaquin and Han sat sweaty in a dimly lit, abandoned garage. Where a personal transport should have been parked was a wasted couch and, on that couch, two wasted men. Joaquin unconsciously reached behind his ear, still expecting the transceiver that sat there for almost five years. Finding nothing, he remembered again—they had taken those out in the forest and left them behind.

If there had been any chance of it until that point, there was no turning back now. Removing a transceiver was punishable with three years. He wondered if he would miss SAI's constant presence and took a moment to appreciate that they were fugitives now. He glanced over at Han who sat catching his breath, drinking one of the water rations stacked against the back wall.

Han, who had tried to warn Joaquin that an officer had stopped by his apartment. Han, who realized something was off when a woman showed up afterward looking for the officer—a woman too pale and too smart to be that kind of a Gamma girl. Han, who set out after his friend at first light and who had likely saved his life.

"Thank you." Joaquin said to Han with deep sincerity.

"You'd do the same for me," Han replied coolly as he got up and ravaged one of the snack rations that sat next to the water stack, on which he had spread his sweat-drenched shirt.

"Wait, you *would* do the same for me, right?" A smile made its way across Han's face as he chewed.

"Maybe." For the first time in days, Joaquin smiled from the bottom of his heart, grateful to have Han as his companion. "So, whose place is this, anyway?"

"My dad's old business partner, Esra. I used to come here as a kid..." Han paused, remembering something that made his eyes glaze nostalgically.

"Esra didn't have any of his own and so sorta spoiled me. When they kicked out all the foreign-borns...well, Esra promised my dad he'd sponsor me so I could stay. He's kept this place stocked since then, just in case." Han took a few steps into the center of the room, his arms and eyes motioning around it.

"And while I know for a *fact* he knows we're here, he's leaving us alone so he doesn't have to lie to anyone in case they track us to this place."

"Han, I had—"

"Look, I don't really want to talk about it. It was a long time ago. And I know Esra is happy to see me taking advantage of his offer from years ago, which makes me happy. Anyway, here's my question for you, boss: now what?"

They both fell silent pondering an answer, then suddenly the side door opened and shut in a blink. On the floor had been placed a device that neither Joaquin nor Han had ever seen, but that they both recognized instantly from stories they'd heard. In the early days of the Transition some people weren't ready to accept wrist implants, and disabling them was cleaner than removing them.

"I told you Esra knows we're here." Han kept his eyes on the bracelet-like device, a chill running down his back as he anticipated what it would do to him. "You first."

Joaquin gave his friend a grimaced look of acknowledgement, then moved to pick up the device from the floor and strap it around his right wrist. He sat back down on the couch, and while his right hand squeezed the sofa cushion his left hand pushed the single button on the device, sending a shock of ten thousand volts searing into his arm. His body twitched, but the pain was less than he'd expected. *As usual.*

"Your turn."

Joaquin unstrapped the device and handed it to Han,

who joined him on the couch. Han strapped on the device, and his index finger hovered above the button. He breathed in, then out, then in, then out. Finally, closing his eyes, he pushed the button and yelped in pain as his body writhed off the couch onto the garage floor. It was over in a few seconds, but to Han it felt like minutes.

"I hate you." Han lay on his back, slowly un-strapping the device, regaining his calm.

Joaquin smiled, and his mind drifted back to the question: *now what?* If Han's surprise at hearing the contents of the card was any indication of how the average Halinite would respond, they absolutely needed to get it to the Cotters, who would know how to disseminate it—and handle the expected government response. To Joaquin, after hearing Natasha's words in the clearing, his intention was evolving beyond just understanding the secrets of the card. It was becoming more about doing what was right. For the first time in as long as he could remember, Joaquin felt...alive.

While Han was less convinced anything could be done— the president always won—he was ready and willing to help Joaquin go as far as he could. He owed him that for the friend Joaquin had been to him over the years—his only true friend who looked past the color of his skin for who he really was. While at first furious at being assigned housing in a Gamma complex given his rank as a Beta-class employee with B1 security clearance, from the day he met his neighbor he'd come to believe there was nowhere else he'd rather live, turning down two subsequent opportunities to upgrade to housing in Beta Ring.

"Well, you're probably right that the Cotters are looking for us, but by now our faces have likely been broadcast across all screens in all Rings. So everyone is looking for us." Joaquin sat, contemplative. "Or maybe not, because the president would want to keep this out of the public eye?"

"No chance your girlfriend can call her mom and get us a pardon, eh? Call the whole thing a misunderstanding?"

Joaquin at first smiled at the jest, but it was brief. Lyla must be worried about him, perhaps even thinking it was somehow her fault. No...she'd be angry at him, more likely. How dare he embarrass her by running away like this? No, she loved him dearly and would be frantic and assuming the worst. Or perhaps she'd just be sad, as he was...

"Stop thinking about her, Joaquin! I'm sorry I said anything," Han cut in. "She's great, but you know she's not great for you. Frankly, at first I thought you were running away from her."

Joaquin gave him a knowing glance.

"Anyway, options. The way I see it we have only one: the Cotters. We can't go to the police because they have kill authorization on you. We can't go to the Resistance, first because we have no idea how to find them, second because we don't know if we can trust them. We can't stay here forever. That leaves the Cotters as our only hope to get out of this mess—question is, how do we find them, or how do they find us, right?

"That's how I see it."

"Well, here's my thought: we go back to the clearing."

"Are you *crazy*?" was Joaquin's first reaction, but as his brain processed the words he immediately recognized it as the only option. He stood. "You're right, you bastard. We have to go back."

"I know. I've known it since we left. Thanks to your 'I have what you're both looking for' line—genius, by the way—the Cotters are wondering what you have that gives an officer authority to kill a relatively law-abiding Gamma-class government employee. They also know what we know, which is that we don't have a lot of time, that we're not safe in any of the Rings on our own, that we wouldn't last more than a few days in a border, and so, that they are our only hope of survival."

Joaquin walked to the stack of water rations and looked around their sanctuary. *How long could we hold out here?* It wasn't really an option, but he pondered the question anyway. With his left hand he reached for a ration, but the watch he had strapped to his wrist caught his eye and he paused. Once again, he had forgotten he was wearing it. The new old device had stopped ticking with the electric jolt, perhaps forever. Joaquin took it off and carefully placed it on the stack, mumbling softly under his breath: "Thank you, Esra."

Joaquin uncapped a water ration, drank it, and put the empty bottle down before yielding to the inevitable. "All right. We go back to the clearing."

He walked back to the couch and took out the card from the book, where it had remained safe, and stared at it. *Where do I hide you?* Joaquin closed his eyes and took a deep breath. Held it. Exhaled. Opening his eyes, he felt energized, and he turned to a half-naked Han. "Do me a favor and put on your shirt."

**

"What the hell happened out there!" The police chief was angry. In all his years of service, Aaren had never seen him get emotional with anyone. It was against their programming, but the chief was old enough that maybe he wasn't engineered? *So this is what that looked like.* "You knew this was a high-priority kill and you let yourself get distracted!"

"Sir, it wasn't a distraction! It was Nata—"

"I don't care if it was the president of Latmero herself, you had an order! And now my boss—our president—is calling *me* asking *me* what *I'm* going to do about it. Do you know what I'm going to do about it?"

"No, sir," was all Aaren had for a reply as he stood there still at attention. The chief usually favored Aaren, always giving him high-profile assignments and strong marks, recognizing his hard work and above-average performance. But not today.

"Well you'd better figure it out. I have four squadrons of incogs and a fleet of scouts combing the streets looking for this guy, but I have a feeling he's smart enough to stay out of sight, so you're going to have to get into his head and figure out where he is."

"Yes, sir."

The police chief sat down with a heavy exhale, his eyes catching a photo on his desk. He turned the frame around to show Aaren.

"Do you recognize these two young soldiers?"

Aaren relaxed and bent to get a closer look at the image. "Is that you, sir?"

"Yes, it is, and that's President Jemmer with me. The frame is nearly thirty years old, when Gaven and I were fresh from officer training, starting our first tour."

"Wow, sir, I didn't know you and the president—"

"There's a lot you don't know, Lieutenant. What worries me is *I* don't know what has the president so worked up. In the thirty years I've known Gaven, I've seen him like this just a handful of times. Just a handful." The police chief stared a moment, caught in a memory.

"Jemmer, you find this Joaquin guy and bring what he stole back to me in the next thirty-six hours and I'll promote you to deputy chief." He paused.

"If someone else finds him with the card and we get this whole thing sorted out, it'll be an honorable discharge."

"Yes, sir."

The chief leaned forward in his chair and his voice turned grave. "But if this card goes public in the next thirty-six hours...son, you'll be branded an accomplice by negligence and be sentenced to death by firing squad."

Aaren paled.

"I like you, Jemmer, you know I do. Don't make me order your execution. Help me promote you to deputy chief. Do I make myself clear?"

"Yes, sir." The words barely left his throat.

"Good. Now go find that sonofabitch."

"Yes, sir!" Aaren sprang to his feet, offered a salute, and darted down the hall to his locker to prepare for his next thirty-six hours. Perhaps his last.

**

Natasha sat at her screen staring at Joaquin's file. Aaren was a lost cause—he'd fired at her!—but Joaquin might be her savior. He was an Archives employee, which meant he had access to restricted materials. She scrolled through his record and logs...a fairly successful career, a markedly loyal citizen. So what did he find that inspired him to throw it all away? Or scared him to do it? Clearly, it was something they were willing to kill him for—and that he was willing to die for. *Unless he doesn't know what he really has?* She let her head fall into her hands and whispered desperately, "Where are you?"

Natasha's mind drifted to Election Day, and she wondered what she would do if the president won by his eighty percent of the electorate margin—a people's mandate. Where could she hide? Her hands moved before her head registered the thought, and she found herself looking at frames of her mother and father.

Her mother speaking at a rally against the wrist implants proposed by the pre-Haline government, her right wrist raised high above the crowd in caution and defiance.

Her mother on the cover of a magazine casting a vote in the Senate for universal access to anti-spore pills. She tapped the image to see the accompanying story:

> *Senator Biron spoke for over an hour in the Senate chambers today pleading for votes in support of her bill. She cited nearly a dozen scientists who had testified in the subcommittee that the microalgae spores causing the country's respiratory issues and related deaths were a direct result of government efforts to engineer a solution to the carbon problem two decades prior...*

She tapped back and saw a frame of her father ruling in favor of a group of farmers who had chosen to grow authentic, heirloom vegetables—and against the government, which had sought to imprison the farmers for violating newly passed agrilaws.

Natasha sighed with a smile, a feeling of pride swelling from her chest out through her fingers and toes. She turned back to Joaquin's file, determined.

9

"There may have been a time, long, long ago, when the ocean provided—but since the shutdown of the flow it has only taken. After decades of bearing the wrath of hurricanes and typhoons slung at them from all sides, our forefathers moved us inland for protection. We may be beyond the reach of her deadliest weapon here in Haline, but even here our Mother Nature, who we poisoned and provoked for hundreds of years, intends to punish us in revenge for hundreds more."

— President Gaven Jemmer, second anniversary of Haline's founding

TWO DAYS UNTIL ELECTION
EVENING, GAMMA / DELTA BORDER

Joaquin and Han approached the clearing, coming in a different way than they had left, just as dusk was settling in. The mosquitoes were hunting in ferocious packs, forcing them to set up a mesh tent and wait for night to fall. While Joaquin was usually left alone by the winged villains, Han was—like most Halinites—a juicy target. They sat there, not a word spoken between them, both wondering the same thing: who would find them first?

They'd spotted an officer standing just outside the clearing, obviously trying not to be obvious. They'd also seen an officer-class personal transport parked in another clearing about a mile away on their approach, so they had to assume there were at least three other officers along with a number of scouts scanning the area. What they hadn't found were any Cotters, or any obvious way to send them a message.

The moon came out bright and just past half-full, casting a soft light over them. Hearing the buzzing of the mosquitoes die down, they began unzipping the mosquito tent, and that's when Joaquin saw it. Just barely, in the dim light, the glint of a camera lens hidden between the branches of a tree. He froze, tapped Han, and pointed to it. They were far enough to the left to not be in view, and a new question was suddenly on both of their minds.

To Joaquin, the answer was clear; why would the government need surveillance out here? Cameras were only used in high-traffic areas—where they were used in abundance—but they wouldn't have one here. Scouts were their roving eyes in the borders. He looked at Han and made a motion with his head that drew a look of concern but not protest. Joaquin turned back toward the camera, took a deep breath, and stepped boldly into its field of view.

Not a second later, Joaquin was tackled from behind and went crashing to the ground, the cold, hard chest plate on his back telling him who had found him first.

"SAI, this is Officer Madden. I have suspect in custody, send rein—ahhh!"

The officer's weight lifted off him and Joaquin rolled over to see Han holding the officer's gun in his hand while kicking the officer in the shins—not getting the expected shrieks of pain but clearly inflicting harm. Satisfied the officer wouldn't be able to chase after them, Han used his free hand to help Joaquin up, and they took off in a sprint away from the clearing, hearing others running in their direction, guns firing.

Seconds later, a massive fireball exploded behind them, sending them flying.

**

Not sure where else to go, Aaren decided to make his way back to the clearing. He knew Joaquin wouldn't dare walk the streets, and Aaren believed the fugitive would continue to try and make contact with the Cotters, the only people who might protect him. He sat quietly in the transport as it sped in the direction of the clearing, his thoughts drifting back to Natasha's words.

I am the son of Cotter parents.

It hung in his mind not nearly as revolting as he thought it might. In fact an odd, deep calm came over him as he accepted the possibility as a probable truth. Deep down, he had more than suspected; he had *known* he wasn't an officer, and Natasha's words answered the question about his past that he had never dared ask. But would they change anything about his future?

Her warnings about the president were likely true, but what did it matter to him? He may have been born a Cotter, but he was raised and had lived like an officer. That's the world he knew. His thoughts vacillated between being thankful to his parents for risking their lives to give him his, and shameful that he was of Cotter blood.

He shook his head to clear his mind, but it flooded with memories of his youth. He had known for a long time that he was not like the other officer boys...

"Aaren! What's wrong with you? Stop your crying."

"But, sir, it hurts...it hurts!" He looked down at his arm where he could see the bone poking in a way he'd never seen it poke before.

"Well if you hadn't fallen off the instaladder like a fool you wouldn't have broken your arm. Now stay still while I set it. And shut your crying...this doesn't hurt nearly as much as it would if you were a regular like me. And I already gave you a painkiller. You shouldn't be feeling a thing."

Aaren forced himself to stop crying, but the pain was excruciating as the doctor reset the bone with the cavalier of having a patient with genetically dulled pain receptors. He could feel himself about to pass out, but before he slipped unconscious a thought flashed in his mind. "But, Doctor, if it does hurt...does that mean I'm a regular?"

"Sir, Officer Madden has found the suspect back at the clearing. We're four minutes away."

Aaren cleared his head. If he didn't get to Joaquin before the Cotters did, it wouldn't matter who he was.

10

"Today I'm excited to share the new Clean Water Pact we've inked with our suppliers that will increase access and lower prices. Long have we lived in dire shortage of this most precious resource, a paradox as it falls from the sky. No longer will our citizens in the outer Rings die from being forced to drink unpurified water."

— President Gaven Jemmer, announcing the Clean Water Pact, second term

TWO DAYS UNTIL ELECTION
NIGHT, EPSILON RING

Joaquin opened his eyes to thick blackness, his nostrils filled with warm, sticky air, his lungs aching for more, his head mildly but distinctly pounding. A few blinks and he realized he was hooded, in a chair, his arms tied behind his back. A fleeting sense of dread passed through him, but he quickly recovered and to his surprise, smiled. If he had been captured by an officer, it would be cold steel hugging his wrists, not the rough texture of worn nylon.

"Han, you here?" he ventured hoarsely, wishing for a water ration.

"Yeah, I think we're going to be fine." Han's reply was quick and betrayed a silent fear, but then again Han hadn't started on his journey prepared for anything like this. He'd only wanted to warn a friend.

The hood came off his head and Joaquin squinted in the

bright beam that hit his eyes from the spotlight facing him from across the room. He closed his eyes, filled his lungs, and then in a tone tinged with expectation, spoke: "Can we get some water, please?"

"Yeah, we can do that. Gini, can you get these guys a couple of water rations?" The voice was strong, measured, and confident. As his eyes adjusted Joaquin made out the face that matched it.

"Who are you and why are you here?" the voice wanted to know.

"Joaquin Deva. And you?"

"I'll ask the questions for now, Mr. Deva. We did save your life, you know. Both of you. That firebomb knocked you and Han out. Another few seconds and the officers would have found you first, and right now you'd be in a cold cell at Central not allowed water, let alone to speak out of turn."

Joaquin noticed that though the voice was rough, the face had a sincerity and kindness about it. But the fact remained that he was tied to a chair.

"How did you get to us so fast? The cam—"

"We had people at the clearing keeping an eye out for you in case you made the mistake of coming back. Do you have any idea how many scouts they had deployed at that location? You're incredibly lucky we found you first. Now answer the question—who are you and why are you here?"

Joaquin calmed. "We know you're Cotters and we risked our lives to find you."

"Or you're government spies sent here to feed us lies, or worse. After all, the Election is only two days away. You do work for the government, do you not, Mr. Deva?"

"The government just tried to *kill* me, as you pointed out. Besides, I'm only a staff employee with G2 security clearance."

"But your friend here, Han Remi, has B1 security clearance. Look, we've pored over your files. We think we know who you are. What we don't know is why two loyal Gamma Ring government employees would be here with something for us."

"Frankly, I don't know why I'm here either." Joaquin's voice slowed. He inhaled deeply. And then let it out: "Forty-eight hours ago I had a great job, a loving girlfriend, a more or less simple life—and now I'm being hunted by the police and sitting here bound at the wrists wondering if you deserve to see what I want to show you."

"What did you come here to show us?" Natasha emerged from the shadows, a tinge of desperation mixed with compassion in her voice. "You were the one the officer was looking for. What do you have that gave him kill auth on you?"

"A datacard. Pre-Haline."

While Joaquin thought he heard a gasp, it was not from her.

"Show me." Natasha's voice was not hopeful, but stern. "Show it to me."

"Uh, hi again." Han sheepishly acknowledged Natasha, thinking back to the circumstances of their first encounter.

"Hello, Han." Natasha's face softened, almost to a smile.

Joaquin paused to look at her. She was beautiful, more so than in the frame in his mind, with her short, brown-black hair cropped close around her face and her light brown eyes. In them he saw compassion...and resolve. He hesitated, appreciating that this was perhaps his last chance to change his mind before officially siding with the Cotters.

"Jacket, left side. There's a loose thread that pulls off to open up a pocket."

Adler walked over to Joaquin and glanced at Natasha for a nod before opening up Joaquin's jacket and finding a seemingly innocent thread poking out from the lining. It could expose a hidden compartment—or it could set off a bodybomb they'd missed in the security sweep. He pulled, and it unraveled to expose a quarter-inch notch. Reaching in with his fingertips, Adler pulled out the thin datacard. After scanning it with his handceiver for a weapon signature or communication signal, he looked to Natasha with hopeful eyes. "It looks pre-Haline, Natasha."

"All right, let's see what we've got." Natasha sat motionless, unconvinced. Perhaps the contents were severe enough to get the attention of the police and merit a kill auth, or perhaps he really was a spy sent as part of a perfectly orchestrated shutdown of the Cotter movement to coincide with the Election. She didn't want to speculate.

Adler turned the datacard to face the wall. "Drop screen," he said, and a large white screen lowered from the ceiling and covered a large portion of the brick wall to the left of where Joaquin and Han were sitting. He turned the datacard toward the screen and pushed the single button.

The datacard turned on, recognized the screen, and began transmitting frames. Within a second the first frame popped up; a harmless-looking image of the ocean. "Scan forward, one frame per second," Adler commanded the card.

The images of the ocean gave way to ones in a presidential conference room with mostly men and a few women looking stern in heated debate. The angles of the photos implied they were candid and the photographer surreptitious, likely using a finger implant. Natasha recognized nothing, but her confidence in the authenticity of the datacard grew with each frame. Something about them seemed raw. And real. The frames moved back to the ocean, and then came the frame of the president with his companion.

"Stop!" Natasha slowly got up from her chair. The frame looked familiar—she remembered the day it was taken—*but she didn't remember it with Gaven Jemmer.*

She looked at Joaquin in a state of complete confusion, and then turned back to the frame. She pictured the day in her mind, a calm summer afternoon of her youth, and a wave of emotion rushed from her heart through her body.

Everything about the photo felt familiar and right—except the face of her pictured companion, who today was known throughout Haline as President Jemmer. She closed her eyes and pictured who it was supposed to be, who she thought— she *knew*—was there with her that day: Ashten, a close friend of her parents who spent time with her whenever he visited them.

Her eyes opened, but as her thoughts began to form into words an alarm went off. The perimeter of the compound had been breached.

**

Aaren stepped into what appeared to be a conference-turned-interrogation room, where two water rations sat half-full on the table. This is the room they had been in when the alarm sounded and they took off in a hurry. No other explanation for abandoned water. He walked the room and in his head tried to recreate what might have happened.

The two chairs in the light were obviously where Joaquin and his companion, Han, had sat; they had deduced the identity of Joaquin's accomplice fairly quickly after their escape from Officer Madden. The chair opposite the table was where one of Natasha's lieutenants, possibly Adler, had begun the questioning. The chair just outside the light—that is where Natasha had been sitting. He kneeled, looking for any sign of struggle on the floor, when his eyes caught a long thread next to one of the chairs. He walked over and it confirmed what he feared; the card, likely concealed in a makeshift pocket the likes of which he'd seen before in his years as an officer, had traded hands. He stood up swiftly and marched out of the room, barking orders to SAI about sending backup and deploying scouts. They were running out of time. *He* was running out of time.

**

Natasha and Adler led a hooded Joaquin and Han through the maze of abandoned point-to-point troop transit tunnels built during the wars. While there had been calls in the early days of Haline to flood the tunnels and "wash away any Resistance and Cotter infestations," the Transport Council had fought to preserve them with hopes of adding lines to the T-sub system in the coming years. Now, Natasha worried the order to flood would come down, fast. She took off Joaquin's hood then turned to Adler. "Hoods off. They're slowing us down."

The four of them picked up the pace and ran another mile of turns and steps before emerging into a wooded area on the edge of a violent rainstorm. In the distance they could see a tornado touching down two or three Rings away, and for a moment Joaquin thought of his friends in Zeta.

Natasha and Adler converted their light jackets into ponchos. With one hand Adler pulled out his ozone balancer and inhaled, and with the other he pulled out an extra acid rain–proof poncho.

"I only have one." He looked from Joaquin to Han.

"You take it, Han." Joaquin walked to an oak tree a few

steps away and broke off a branch with some leaf cover that he raised above his head. "Where to now?"

Natasha put her hood on, turned to Joaquin with a look of subtle admiration, and then turned back out to the clearing where in the distance they could make out a structure next to the curve of the tree line.

"We jog the edge of the trees another mile. We have a friend waiting for us. Let's go."

Natasha took off to her right, hugging the tree line to stay as dry as possible while keeping a wary eye on the tornado that seemed to be coming closer. They reached a house and a barn, where a man beckoned them frantically as if the mere action of waving his arm would move them more quickly indoors.

They disappeared into the barn, and the man disappeared into the house. Natasha led them to a compartment in the middle of the stable, where they sat with horses on every side and a holomirror at the center. Anyone—or any scout—looking casually would assume there was no place for anything else. There was a latched floor door that Joaquin assumed was there "just in case."

Fifteen minutes passed without a word. The only sounds were of drumming rain and rolling thunderclaps as the water and sweat slowly dried in the heat of the insulated barn. After taking several minutes to appreciate the horses— he had never seen one in the flesh—Han stretched out awkwardly in the tight space and nodded off. Adler meditated, his back straight as a board, his breath calm and measured, his legs crossed. Natasha sat pondering the frame and noticing Joaquin's occasional glances. He clearly sought acceptance or encouragement or thanks, or perhaps simple acknowledgement, but her mind was obsessed and she paid no attention.

She closed her eyes, her brow furrowed. *That is me, but that is not Ashten. And it was Ashten, right?* Her memory, usually sharp, was fuzzy around aspects of her youth. It was as if a filter had been placed over certain days of her childhood, leaving her with only feelings and images. Cloudy glimpses into her past. She thought she was merely suppressing the days of darkness around the time her mother died, but perhaps...

Ashten. It was Ashten. She was sure, but she wasn't. Not anymore.

She let out a sigh and opened her eyes, letting her gaze fall on Joaquin, who was staring at her. He immediately looked away but let his eyes slowly return.

"It is you in that frame, right?" He spoke as softly as a falling leaf.

She paused. Then slowly, "Yes, it's me."

"And your companion—"

"Was not the president." Her whisper had edges.

"Oh," was all Joaquin could muster before he too closed his eyes, straining to remember the frame.

She continued, "But in the photo, it appears he was

there. My…companion. And that's what I can't figure out."

"What do you mean?"

"I'm not sure what I mean."

"So…" Joaquin wanted to continue the conversation but realized from her tone he'd get nowhere pursuing the details around the frame. "You've seen the ocean?"

"Many times, yes…growing up my father would take me there as often as he felt was safe, once every year or so." Natasha paused and suddenly realized she was glad to have someone to share her heavy thoughts with.

"Ashten was a friend of my parents who would visit us from time to time, and I have few but fond memories of him. He would come by the house, and my parents would embrace him with a love so pure that I loved him instinctively, even though I barely knew him." She paused, remembering.

"The frame is one of my last memories of Ashten, a day we went out to the cliffs. It wasn't long after that my mother died. For whatever reason Ashten never came by again after that. I haven't really thought about him since."

"Could the frame be forged?" Joaquin asked, his voice a blend of fear and anticipation.

"It's possible, but how? Why? No, I don't think so. The other frames seem authentic, as does the card itself. And that's what has me so…scared."

"What? What has you scared?"

"If the frame is real, then my memories are not."

part two

11

They were on the move again, underground, making their way from the Delta Ring into the Beta Ring; for what purpose or reason, Joaquin had no idea. Back at the barn after a short night of uncomfortable sleep, Adler and Natasha left Joaquin and Han for about half an hour—undoubtedly to plan—and since then had spoken little to them. With the datacard firmly in Natasha's possession and Joaquin and Han clearly slowing them down, Joaquin wondered why they were being brought along at all. He naively hoped it was because they were part of the team now. He secretly feared it was because they made good hostages.

Their pace had slowed as they navigated the maze of tunnels and stairwells of the abandoned transit system, and the silence had become almost awkward. Joaquin brought himself alongside Natasha.

"Hey. So…I'm guessing you're still not sure if you can

trust us." Joaquin's voice betrayed a frustration that surprised him. "And I'm pretty sure the only reason you're bringing us along is so you can trade us in if things go south. But you have to know by now that there's no way we're incogs or anything like that. And after the sacrifices we've made to bring you this profound discovery that might help you finally see some success after years of obscurity and failure, I think we deserve more."

The words pierced sharply, but Natasha kept walking, not turning her head to hear him, not taking her eyes off the ground ahead of her feet. Adler and Han followed closely within earshot, and Adler nervously wondered what Natasha would say. She let several minutes pass before she replied.

"These tunnels were built during the wars. Some by the militia that attacked from the outside. Some by the factions of the army and police that fought each other on the inside. Few Halinites know they still exist."

Natasha raised her eyes to Joaquin and saw his suspicion and doubt.

"You don't know anything about me, do you?"

Joaquin wanted to be angry at the change in subject, but the new topic fascinated him. "No. Actually I don't."

Natasha walked a few steps before continuing.

"They actually contacted me. The early Cotters, I mean." Natasha turned her head to Joaquin. "I was forging a life as an architect at the time. Anyway, I saw Gaven Jemmer like most others did when he came to power—a bit of a godsend, you know? He brought order to the chaos."

She smiled, remembering how she used to feel about him in those days. How everyone felt about him in those days. Hopeful.

"When he held the first Election to legitimize the position he'd taken by military force, I was impressed. But then a few months after the Election his restrictive laws 'to protect and to serve' began rolling out, and I grew angry." She paused but Joaquin remained silent. She continued.

"I suppose it was because my parents were such strong advocates of citizen rights in the pre-Haline government. They would have been furious about the price of Jemmer's so-called peace. So I started graffiting the very buildings I had helped design with choice words about Jemmer, and shortly after, the Cotters sought me out and invited me in. I was wary at first but then..." As they walked a few paces without words, the sound of gravel beneath their feet seemed loud.

"And then they told me...showed me...that my parents had been killed by the people who had put Jemmer into power."

"No!" Joaquin stopped walking, but Natasha strolled casually forward.

"I'd always wondered, even suspected, but to know...to know, that was different. At first I was angry and wanted nothing to do with the Cotters or anyone, but after a few weeks I closed my architecture business, moved out of my apartment, and joined them."

Joaquin glanced back at Han and caught Adler's eyes, but few words came to him as he looked back on Natasha. "I'm—"

"Not two months later I was leading their...*our* fight against the president's proposed 'Safety First' agenda. That was a disaster." Natasha shook her head.

"What do you mean?"

"The people of Haline were still scared. Safety First meant security at any cost. Our efforts to rally support against the Act were futile next to fresh, painful pre-Haline memories." She turned to Joaquin. "You remember the wars."

Joaquin's mind went back to that morning by the ocean's shore holding his uncle's hand, and then to the shots that rang out in their direction. His uncle picked him up and, sheltering him, ran them back to their personal transport, fortunately parked behind a massive rock. His uncle opened Joaquin's door first and rushed him in. As he shut the door his uncle yelped in pain, a splash of blood hitting the window. Joaquin screamed, his hand on the window and his eyes welling with tears. His uncle looked down at his pierced hand, then quickly rounded the transport and painfully drove them out to safety and then home. It was one of the few times the violence of the wars had touched Joaquin's life, but it was vivid and sharp. And it still hurt.

"Yes, I remember," was all he offered.

"The people ended up being thankful for it." Natasha didn't have to explain what 'it' was; the Safety First Act was now a part of everyday life on Haline—SAI, an ever-present network with ubiquitous surveillance and reach, police-enforced curfews and strict travel restrictions between Rings, an outer wall that isolated Haline from the rest of the world, government-issued wrist implants and transceivers.

"Now, just five years later, the president is on the verge of dissolving Congress."

"No!" Joaquin remembered hearing something about Congress at the clearing, but the words that reached his ears were faint. *What would happen to Lyla's mother?*

The more he learned, the more Joaquin found that his growing fear felt more like anger, focused on a single face— the face in the frame next to Natasha's at the ocean.

"Without a Congress to check his power, Gaven Jemmer will tighten his grip. You'll see higher food prices. Anti-spore pill rationing. Water shortages. And worse. Of course, he'll also have us Cotters hunted down and imprisoned, exiled, or killed." Natasha inhaled audibly.

They walked along in silence, both with eyes on the ground.

"Joaquin, we're going to a broadcast station in Alpha where Adler is going to try and upload the frames off of the card onto an emergency broadcast signal."

"Wha…" Joaquin's pathetic reply matched the jolted expression on Han's face. If Adler and Natasha succeeded in getting even a few of the key frames pushed to every screen in Haline this close to the Election…

"There's no way they're going to let you." Han's mind had raced forward, his years of communications expertise spinning in his head as he plotted out all possible outcomes.

"They have to know that you're going to try to broadcast. It's the worst-case scenario for what you could do with media like that. They'll have firewalls protecting access to the broadcast towers so thick even SAI might not have access. And if you think you're going to be able to break into a studio and do it from a key terminal, you either have people on the inside—which I doubt—or are resigned to go down as martyrs." Han paused a second. "Wait, is that it? Is this a glorified suicide mission?"

"No, Han, it's not." It was Adler who spoke this time. "Give us some credit, will you? We don't need to get on every screen. Just enough of them so that it causes the confusion needed to postpone the Election. Jemmer will undoubtedly suspend voting once results are affected, and that will be our opportunity to get the support we need to mount a counter-campaign with the rest of the images on the datacard."

He paused to glance at Natasha, who nodded. He continued: "Central Studio has six fiber lines that lead away from the building, one for each Ring, as a backup to central tower coverage. If we can hack just one of the six, it should be enough. I just hope I can do it."

"What do you mean?" Han was unconvinced, but played along.

"Gini is our resident comm expert, but it's too risky to get her to meet us in Alpha all the way from Epsilon. If I fail, we can possibly try something again tomorrow. If I contact her and they hack my line, or she gets caught en route, everything will unravel."

Joaquin threw Han a knowing glance and let out a quiet sigh of relief. Communications was Han's area of expertise, and tapping a fiber line to override central broadcast was something he was certain Han had done before. They weren't going to be hostages for much longer. They'd be teammates after all.

Before Joaquin calmed, there was one more question he had to ask. "Natasha, which studio are we going to?"

"Central Studio. Where your girlfriend Lyla works."

A wave of emotion passed through Joaquin, but he said nothing. He should have figured as much. It explained why Natasha took the time to share her story and the president's plans for Congress. *Damn, what have I gotten myself into? At least Lyla will be home with her mother. Unless...*

"In about an hour, we'll go topside and hack a terminal so you can contact her anonymously." Natasha stopped and turned to Joaquin, extending a hand to his shoulder. "I wish we didn't have to get her involved, but we need them to think we're trying to break into the studio itself. It's the only way they'll possibly overlook a spike in traffic from one of the fiber lines for long enough to matter. If we get her to the studio it'll be enough to tip off Aaren."

Seeing worry spread across Joaquin's face, Natasha put her other hand on his other shoulder. "She won't be in any danger whatsoever at any time, I promise you that. If nothing else she's the congressional leader's daughter, and Jemmer hasn't taken absolute control just yet."

Joaquin held her eyes a moment as he ran through his options. He had none.

**

Aaren glanced at the inside of his wrist. Twenty-three hours until he was either promoted, relieved, or sentenced for execution. He stood in his office at headquarters, wary of the chief's eyes on his back as he evaluated a live holomap of the Haline populace as assembled by SAI and transceiver data. He'd run dozens of queries, but each one netted out the same—nothing. Aaren sat down, closed his eyes, and worked to collect his thoughts, reminding himself of everything he knew.

One: Natasha would attempt to disseminate the contents of the datacard. Whatever was on there, it was severe enough that the president himself was involved, so it was likely that a little would go a long way. Even if people didn't believe its authenticity, it would cause enough confusion to affect the Election. Not that the president had any chance of losing, but he wouldn't win by the margin he wanted to do whatever it was he had planned. *And I wouldn't be around to see it, whatever it is.*

Two: they have no chance at hacking broadcast signals from a tower, so they'll go after a hard line. There were about two dozen studios spread across the six Rings, and any one of them would allow them the broadcast range they needed. Yes, he had incogs positioned in every one of them now—uniformed officers would scare them off and Aaren would miss his chance to catch them—but Natasha *could* bypass the studios altogether and settle for a smaller burst from a single terminal anywhere in Haline. If she chose that path, Aaren could contain the damage by having SAI and scouts at the ready.

Three: the best place to do the *most* damage would be from Central Studio, but they'd be foolish to think they could get in. Still, something told Aaren that that was in fact where they were heading. That was where Joaquin's girlfriend worked, and more importantly, Natasha wouldn't risk a small, potentially ineffective burst. She'd undoubtedly want broad exposure for maximum impact, even if she and her team were killed in the process. For the first time in as long as she'd been leading the Cotters, the scales massively tilted in her favor, and he knew she would not let the opportunity be missed.

Aaren opened his eyes back to the map and zeroed in on Central Studio. *As crazy as it is for them to think they'll succeed, that is where they are heading.* He jumped up, snapped on his minmax vest, and ran out the door to his transport, calling Central Studio and asking them to create a subtle security gap where Natasha might think she could get through to the hard lines. Nothing obvious, but something she would think she discovered and was her window. And then when she went through that window, he'd be there to catch her.

Minutes after leaving headquarters Aaren's transceiver rang. It was his chief.

"Sir, I was just about to update you. I know where they're—"

"You're relieved of your command, Aaren."

Aaren felt his stomach tighten and his heart drop.

"But sir, I still have over twenty-two hours, and I know—"

"It wasn't my call, Jemmer. The president is taking over this operation himself. God knows why, but he's en route to Central Studio where he thinks they're heading and plans to intercept them. He's brought in his guard to complement our incogs. I'm not supposed to be telling you this, but I want you to know how serious this is. I have no damn clue what's on that datacard but whatever it is it's now a blasted national emergency, albeit a private one. Mums the word, of course. SAI is making sure no communication about any of this gets out."

"Sir, I'm minutes away from the studio and I know—"

"You're relieved, Aaren, and are ordered back to HQ where I'm supposed to sit on you until this blows over.

Assuming the president recovers this datacard—and with the amount of manpower he's putting into it I'm damn sure he will—you should end up with a decent place out in Zeta with a sizeable annual pension. Don't throw that away and get yourself killed. Turn around—"

"I'm losing you, sir. It must be the electromagnetic field around the studio power pods disrupting—"

"Dammit, Jemmer—"

"Sorry, sir. I can't hear you."

Aaren pulled over a few blocks away from Central Studio. Just as he was closing the transport door the transceiver he left behind on the seat started emitting a hypersonic pulse. The waves penetrated through the vehicle and passed through Aaren, who was oblivious and unaware. He jogged away from the transport toward the T-sub stop on the other side of the power pods.

12

"Lyla, it's me." Joaquin was standing at a terminal in Alpha with Adler just behind him inhaling from his ozone balancer. Adler had hacked a SAI-free line to Lyla while Natasha and Han remained underground in the tunnel next to the T-sub station entrance three hundred feet away.

"Joaquin! Oh my God...where have you been? What happened to you? Please tell me you're okay—"

"Baby, I'm fine. I'm sorry I didn't call earlier. I've had to...remove my transceiver. This is a clean line. SAI can't hear us. It's a long story but I'm fine."

"What? Where are you?"

"Honey, I can't tell you that, but listen closely—we don't have a lot of time and I need your help with something."

"I don't understand, Joaquin, what are you talking about? Where are you?"

"Lyla, listen to me. First of all, I need you to know that

everything is going to be fine. Can you repeat that back to me?" Emotion crept into Joaquin's voice, but he closed his eyes and pushed it down. He had to stay focused. And they had to get back underground as quickly as possible.

"I...yes. Everything is going to be fine."

"Okay. Listen carefully and don't react."

"Yes...okay...tell me."

"I'm being...detained by the Cotters."

"What?!"

"Babe, it's not like we've heard. They're good and decent people and I'm perfectly safe. But listen, they...we need you to come down to the office, your office, at Central."

"Joaquin, I don't know what they've done to you but my mother has connections and can—"

"No, Lyla, listen. Keep your mom out of this, for her sake, your sake, and my sake. Just you. Just come down to Central. Don't tell anyone we spoke and don't be odd about it. Come get something you left at the office that you need for vacation. A jacket or something. Do you have something you can pick up?"

"Ummm...yeah...I did leave my running shoes at the office, but—"

"Perfect Lyla, perfect. Just head to the office, pick them up, and then take them home. That's it. I can't tell you why you need to do it, but I can tell you that if you do and are normal about it like you just forgot your shoes at the office, everything is going to be fine." Joaquin hated lying, and what was worse was he knew that she knew he was lying, but he had no choice. *How could everything possibly be fine?*

"Okay...I'll do it...I'm worried about you, baby. I love you."

Joaquin paused. "I love you too, Lyla."

He had never truly felt or said those words before, but at that moment he did both. Adler reached over and terminated the line then pulled Joaquin away toward the T-sub station. "We gotta go, now."

They rejoined Natasha and Han underground after passing hurriedly through the station, mildly disguised with dashglasses that falsified their iris patterns and hats pulled down over their faces. Together, the four of them navigated another half mile to a crossroads in the tunnels just a few hundred feet from Central Studio. Adler took a scancam out and examined the area. It identified the bulge in the building that signified the root of the fiber lines.

"It looks like the closest line crosses about ten feet straight through this wall." Adler nodded toward his right while putting the scancam away, then looked at Natasha with uncomfortable eyes. "Ready?"

"Yes." Natasha turned to Han and Joaquin. "We're going to tunnel through to the line, but you two are not coming with us." Adler took out his gun, set it to minimum stun, and pointed it at Joaquin.

Joaquin couldn't believe his ears or his eyes, and he

heard Han yelp then cover his mouth with his hand.

"If we get caught it'll be safer for you two back here. When they find you stunned they'll assume you accompanied us under duress."

"Wait. Don't do this. You need us."

"You've already done enough, and if something should happen to us you should know how deeply thankful I am for taking the risk you took and giving us this opportunity. This last chance."

"I didn't do it for you, but that doesn't matter. Natasha, one of the people you're pointing a gun at has tapped a fiber line before." Joaquin's voice was surprisingly calm for having a gun pointed at him. "And frankly, he's your only chance at doing it right the first time."

It took Han a second to understand that Joaquin was talking about him, and he realized that in all their years of friendship Joaquin had never paid attention to him when Han explained what he did—network design, not hardware. Math, not engineering. But now didn't seem like the right time to correct him.

Natasha looked at Han. "You've done this before?"

Han hesitated, glanced at Joaquin with an odd look, and lied: "Yes, yes I have. It's actually not that hard. Maybe Adler can do it and I can supervise." Han peeked again at Joaquin then back at Natasha.

Natasha pondered a moment and then decisively continued, her voice flat. "Fine. Han can stay here and help.

But then, Joaquin, I have another idea for you," and she held out her gun for him to take as Adler lowered his.

"They'll be expecting someone to show up at Central Studio, and if no one does they might start wondering. I need you to go another two hundred yards or so down the tunnel then up the first exit shaft you see. It should put you on the edge of the square near the studio. It's a short five-minute walk from there, though I expect they'll get to you before you get there. If you don't fire at them they won't fire at you, but if you don't have a gun they won't believe—"

"Natasha, no *way*. You heard what Aaren said in the clearing. He had kill authority on me. I know what's on the datacard, remember? They'll—"

"They won't touch you until they're sure they can get to us and recover the card." She paused. "Joaquin, there's no safer place for you in the world right now than out there, *without* us. I promise you that."

"What if you fail and I'm put behind bars? What then?" Joaquin wasn't convinced.

"We'll come get you. We've gotten our people out before."

"What if you...can't come get me." The words came out in a stutter.

Natasha caught his meaning. "Someone will get you. The folks back at HQ know you're with us."

Joaquin looked at her a second longer, then slowly took the gun from her hand. He'd never held a handgun before—

let alone an officer-class minmax—and it was lighter than he expected. His fingers played on it as he turned it over. Natasha reached out and put her hand over his.

"Hold it like this. This is the safety here, and this is the min stun, max stun, kill switch here," Natasha pointed. "Right now it's on max stun and the safety is on. Just hold it in your hand and be ready to put it down when they tell you to."

The feeling that came over Joaquin at Natasha's touch was familiar. She removed her hand but remained close, and he stood without reply. Natasha looked up and for the briefest of moments they held each other's eyes.

Lowering her head and taking a step back, Natasha continued: "If all goes to plan, we'll be at the fiber in about five minutes. It won't take more than a minute or two to tap it, and then we'll make a run for it. I can't tell you where we're going in case they drug you, which is the worst they would do, but we will find you. If this works, you'll be a hero to the people for your bravery."

"I told you, I wasn't trying to be brave. I just wanted to understand."

"Well, do you?"

"Not at all."

They both smiled knowing and painful smiles, and again their eyes met in a moment of their own. Then she sent him off. "Good luck, Joaquin. Now get out of here."

Joaquin shifted his gaze to Han, who stood with moist

eyes. They embraced, and Han held on and held tight. Parting, they nodded, and Joaquin turned to continue down the tunnel.

"All right, Han, why don't you go stand around the corner that way. Our digdev is quick and relatively quiet, but it does kick back a lot of dirt. How much longer, Adler?"

"I'll be ready here in just a second. The digdev is saying it's four and a half minutes to the fiber."

Adler had been setting up the digdev by attaching it to the wall, and he began programming the diameter and depth of the desired tunnel. He finished, gave a glance backward to make sure everyone was a safe distance away, punched "GO," and then took several hurried steps back himself. The digdev began humming at a low intensity as it warmed up—a sound that seconds later was silenced by another; a gunshot shattered the digdev into several pieces and it clattered on the floor.

13

20 HOURS UNTIL ELECTION
AFTERNOON, ALPHA RING

"Natasha, Adler, guns down. Do it now." Aaren emerged from a shadow, his gun raised and aimed squarely at Natasha. He moved slowly, deliberately.

"No." It was more a whimper than a reply. Natasha stood staring at the device now in pieces across the floor.

"No," she said again, this time louder. Turning just her head, she looked at Aaren with a mixture of sadness and disbelief.

"I said guns down, Natasha."

Natasha held his eyes as her emotions moved between anger and focused calm. "Aaren...you...Aaren, I knew your parents."

"Even if you did, it doesn't matter. What matters is now, and right now I'm an officer and you're under arrest."

As Natasha regained her calm, details emerged as she grasped the situation. Aaren was alone. *Why was he alone?* "Aaren, where's your transceiver?"

Aaren remained silent.

Natasha's voice strengthened as she took a step toward Aaren. "And your backup? Scouts?"

Aaren stood firm.

Natasha continued: "You were relieved of duty for not stopping us in the clearing, weren't you. I'm not surprised...in fact, I'll bet the president himself is involved, given what's on this datacard. You failed, Aaren, and after nearly a lifetime of service, how did your superiors treat you? They abandoned you."

"If I'm to believe you, my parents abandoned me, and I turned out just fine. I guess I'm getting used to it." Aaren moved his gun from Natasha to Han. "Natasha, do as I say or Han dies. It's over, can't you see that?"

"It isn't over." Joaquin emerged from the shadow across the tunnel, his gun squarely pointed at Aaren. "Put your gun down, Aaren."

Aaren pivoted his aim to Joaquin. "Joaquin, stand down. You're out of your league."

Joaquin continued inching toward Aaren, his gun fixed in aim, his eyes fixed in focus. "Natasha?"

"Don't even think about reaching for your weapons." Aaren held his mark on Joaquin.

"Aaren, listen to me. You and I both know the consequences of this Election if Jemmer wins by the margin he's planning for." Natasha's voice had regained its full strength.

"It doesn't concern me."

"Maybe not today, but it will. If Congress is dissolved, genetic design will accelerate. It's likely that they'll even reinstate treatments, something we haven't seen since the wars but something the president will need to maintain his control over Haline police as his fist clenches tighter."

Natasha paused to make sure Aaren paid close attention to where she was going. "Sooner or later, they will start treating officers."

Aaren remained quiet, but beads of sweat began gathering on his brow and his face reflected the torment on his mind. *Is she right? Is it just a matter of time?* Aaren broke eye contact from Joaquin toward Natasha.

Before he realized it was happening Joaquin squeezed the trigger and the gun fell from Aaren's hand.

"Ah! You bastard!" Aaren fell to his knees grasping his hand. The electric pulse from the tiny bullet was absorbed by his vest, but the impact of a max stun shot at close range pierced the flesh of Aaren's palm, and the ensuing pain seared through his whole body. Natasha and Adler quickly withdrew their guns, and Natasha kicked Aaren's weapon away from him before grabbing his other gun from his belt.

"Joaquin! Where did that come from?" Han's heart still beat with the intensity of seconds before having had a gun pointed at it. His face, however, had moved from mortal fear to sheer euphoria. He took a step toward Joaquin, who had lowered his gun and was gently placing it on the floor with the fascination of holding something immensely powerful, extremely delicate, and not at all understood. He looked up just as Han threw his arms around his savior.

"I don't know how you did that, but my God it was beautiful." Han stepped back and then hugged a shaken Joaquin a second time.

Natasha pulled Aaren's hands behind his back, carefully handling the wound, and tied a nylon rope around them while Adler worked to bind his feet. Aaren writhed in revolt but quickly realized it to be pointless and acquiesced to save his energy, the shame of his failure almost more painful in his heart than the burn on his hand. Natasha bent on one knee next to him, took out a handkerchief, and began tying a knot around his palm to stop the bleeding.

"You should have heard the way you screamed. Officers don't scream. Their pain receptors have been dulled—but you..." Natasha leaned in close. "You are not an officer. You are one of us."

She finished tying the knot and brushed some dirt off of Aaren's forehead. "I'm truly sorry that you've lived a lie your whole life. What you've had to endure to make it this far I can only imagine."

She looked at Aaren with sympathy. He stared down at the floor as she spoke, avoiding her gaze—then raised his eyes to hers and opened his lips as if to speak, but closed them and looked back down to the floor. There was nothing he could say that would matter. Nothing mattered, anymore.

Natasha stood and turned to her team.

"What now?" Han asked the obvious question on everyone's mind. To whom he asked the question was equally obvious.

"I don't know." Natasha looked to Adler, who shook his head. She turned to Joaquin. "Where did you learn to shoot like that?"

Joaquin chuckled, the shock having given way to elation. "When I was a kid my uncle taught me to hunt the rats that would nest around his property. But...that was ages ago. And with a small rifle, not a minmax. Honestly, it was a lucky shot."

Adler smiled. "Aim is something you learn for life, Joaquin. You must have put down a good number of rats in—"

They came in from every shadow, over a dozen of them, each in Citizen Guard military drab and each with a gun squarely pointed at Natasha, Han, Adler, or Joaquin, who slowly, instinctively, raised their hands above their heads. Aaren's head moved back and forth, and then his eyes grew wide.

"Nice work, Lieutenant. And without a moment to spare, eh?" President Jemmer strolled in, his hands clasped behind his back. His eyes went to the shattered digdev on the floor, and then he walked up to Natasha and smiled, lingering a moment. He turned to look at Adler, then Han, then Joaquin.

"Mr. Deva, you've been the cause of some unnecessary excitement the past day or so. I assure you, you'll find it wasn't worth it. Not in the slightest." The president returned his gaze to Aaren.

"Clever of you, Lieutenant, to defy the orders of your superior, knowing full well that under the circumstances it would require him to track you down and extrapolate your course of action. If you had told us this plan of theirs we wouldn't have believed you—so you decided to show us. Well done."

Gaven Jemmer turned to a member of his Citizen Guard. "Untie him and get him on his feet. I'd like him to personally arrest this bunch so they can all savor what was truly inevitable, no matter how hard they attempted to evade it."

Aaren's mind scrambled; he had in fact *not* known that "under the circumstances" it would be a priority to track him down. Knowing the likely outcome when he was found, he never would have risked it. Surely the president knew he had left his transceiver behind? He in fact didn't *want* to be found for fear of being empty handed. He turned to the president as the binds came off his wrists and ankles. "Thank you, sir. I told you I wouldn't let you down."

Gaven gave Aaren a look full of words that only Aaren would understand while he slowly mouthed, "Indeed."

He turned to Natasha. "In any case, let's get this lot to the brig at Central. Once night falls I want them transferred to Bunker One. Can you take over from here, Lieutenant?"

"Yes, sir. It'll be done." Aaren clicked his heels and gave his commander in chief a tight salute, his hand wrapped in Natasha's handkerchief and a thick drop of blood slowly moving down his cocked wrist, leaving a trail of red.

"Very good." Gaven returned to the shadow from which he had emerged, leaving behind several of his personal CG force to support Aaren.

14

19 HOURS UNTIL ELECTION
LATE AFTERNOON, ALPHA RING

As critical points for disseminating information to the Haline populace, security at broadcast studios was tighter than the average government office. Accordingly, they had been designed with holding cells for any would-be perpetrators.

Natasha, Han, Joaquin, and Adler were ushered into Central's single cell at gunpoint, and in a mixed state of exhaustion and depression each took a seat on the concrete floor, their backs to the concrete wall, saying nothing.

"Don't get too comfortable. We'll be moving you in about an hour." Aaren's tone was softer than Natasha remembered it being earlier, but she assumed it was because the president had the datacard and she was sitting behind bars—not because any of her words had had an effect on the officer.

Not two minutes after Aaren walked out did Lyla rush in, fresh tear trails on her cheeks, her hands red and black and orange and blue, blistered with burns. "Joaquin!"

"Lyla!" He unfolded his legs and ran to the bars, his hands reaching for hers but pulling back as she got closer.

"Lyla! What have they done!?" Anger boiled in Joaquin as he tried to understand her hands, which she held tenuously in front of her. She moved her lips through the bar and Joaquin met her there for only a second before leaning back and demanding, "My God...Lyla, talk to me...*what did they do to your hands?*"

"They...Joaquin...I can't, I don't want to talk about it. They promised they're going to take me home now but they had questions about you...all these questions about you and..."

"Go on, Lyla."

She shook her head as she held back a sob. "I can't...I just want to forget. Baby, what did you do?"

"Nothing! I mean...nothing wrong. I did nothing wrong, Lyla. But it's going to be fine. You're going to be fine, okay?"

"Joaquin, when I got here to pick up my shoes, there was someone waiting for me and he told me that you were a suspect of some kind and they needed to detain me. And then they took me to a room..."

"I'm sorry, Lyla..." Joaquin buried his head in his chest and leaned into the bars, grasped the situation, then took a deep breath—and control of his anger. It dissipated but left behind a thick residue he did not recognize, and Joaquin felt something inside of him he had never felt before.

"I'm fine...it's just my hands. But I'll be okay. I'm just so worried...Joaquin, what are they going to do to you?"

"I can't explain now, but it'll all be okay. Lyla, I'll *never* forgive them for touching you." His teeth clenched, and he again willed himself to calm.

Lyla's eyes shifted from deep concern to profound fear and she shook her head. "Joaquin, I should go." She inhaled to catch a sob. "I should go."

Joaquin's heart sank, though he wasn't sure if it was because he felt abandoned, or misunderstood, or angry, or just sad. Summoning his greatest self he took a deep breath, closed his eyes, and then replied: "I understand, Lyla."

He opened his eyes and continued, "Please take care of yourself. Just stay with your mother until this is behind us. I'm so sorry for anything they did to you." He moved toward the bars, his arms grasping her waist.

"I'll be fine, Joaquin, just...just..." She was about to start crying again, and the back of her left wrist went to her mouth. With a shake of her head and her eyes welling up, she turned to run out of the room, pausing at the door to look back at Joaquin for a moment before she disappeared.

Joaquin stood there, his own hands still through the bars, his eyes on the empty doorway.

"My God, I'm so, so sorry, Joaquin." Natasha's voice was tight with emotion. A moment passed before she continued. "I'm sorry I asked you to involve her and I'm sorry things turned out the way they did..."

Joaquin remained still while his eyes moved slowly from the doorway to his hands. He willed his lingering anger to cool, and he was suddenly overcome with an odd feeling of relief. In the last thirty-six hours his world had changed entirely, and Joaquin realized he was no longer in any position to be good to her—or for her. Suddenly he missed Lyla with such a depth of loss that he knew she would not ever be coming back. And though he wasn't ready yet to admit it, he knew it was for the best.

"It's not your fault, Natasha." Joaquin finally replied, turning around. "It's mine. And while I will never forgive them—" the emotion boiled back up, he caught it, and let it out in a breath, "for what they did to Lyla, she's a tough girl. But they crossed a line, Natasha." He shook his head. "They crossed a line."

"Joaquin." It was barely a whisper, but it was all Adler could say. SAI was in the room, and she watched every word, every movement, every expression.

Natasha sat there, dumbfoundedly staring at her past, uncomfortably predicting her future, and not believing her present. She vacillated between feelings of anger and defeat, calm and control—and then focused on a single wish: if only she had a plan. But she had no plan.

In her mind's eye Natasha pictured Election Day proceeding as President Jemmer planned, millions of voters electing their own enslavement. She shuddered at the thought.

"My uncle used to have this phrase…" Joaquin could stand the silence no longer. "When life fights you till you have nothing left, take strength from knowing many fight with less."

"I'm not sure I know how to fight anymore, Joaquin. Nor who to fight. Or even…what I'm fighting for." Natasha's voice sounded weak and wasted.

"What do you mean?"

"I…I can't explain right now." Natasha turned a quick eye to the camera mounted on the wall directly opposite the cell.

"Can't explain what?" Aaren marched in, a hard look spread across his face, determination in his stride.

Natasha said nothing, but Joaquin had words as he sat up and walked to the bars: "*You*. Were *you* the one who ordered them to torture Lyla?"

"No…what? No…I don't know what you're talking about."

"Her hands. They *burned her hands.*"

Aaren shook his head in open-mouthed denial. "I'm so sorry about that, Joaquin, but I assure you I had nothing to do with it."

Joaquin felt the anger in him soften slightly at an apology that he believed sincere, and he went to sit back down against the wall.

Turning to the two CG soldiers sitting in the far corner of the room, Aaren commanded, "Leave us."

They looked at each other, and one opened his mouth as if to protest, but the other stood and with a "Yes, sir," got up to leave the room, the other following him with a scowl.

Aaren waited for SAI to slide the door closed behind them before he moved to the camera on the far wall and pushed a button that turned the steady green light to an intermittent soft blue. He then reached behind his ear and muttered, "SAI, logging off," before removing his replacement transceiver and putting it on the table next to the door. Grabbing a chair, Aaren walked toward the cell, setting it down and then sitting down in it.

He waited. Natasha, Adler, Joaquin, and Han waited. Finally Aaren spoke. "Tell me about my parents."

All eyes turned to Natasha, who donned a look of pleasant surprise. She inhaled deeply, looked about her, then up at the camera with the blinking blue light, and then back at Aaren. He would never have spoken those words if they were not completely alone. She exhaled.

"They were doctors, Aaren. Soel worked in genetics on the officer program, while Alyel worked in the emergency room, both at Central. They met in medical school during the wars and afterward worked tirelessly for the people. I met them only once, with my father. They were friends, our fathers, both working for a government they believed could be salvaged on behalf of a people who needed to be served."

"Why did they abandon me?"

"They *saved* you, Aaren. My God, don't you remember

what it was like during the wars? I suppose you were shielded in training, unaware of the suffering beyond your insulated world. Working in the hospital, your parents knew more than most about the severity of the times. Your mother especially, I imagine, being in the emergency room. Surely it was not an easy or thoughtless decision but something they likely weighed back and forth for months. Think about how much planning and work it must have been for you to be born in the regular nursery and then smuggled *into* the officer's nursery? Under constant surveillance and guard?" She paused and stared at the far wall, softly shaking her head in disbelief before continuing.

"They wanted you to live in safety and comfort, Aaren, which was not a life they believed they could offer you."

Aaren's eyes had drifted from Natasha to his hands, which clasped each other in his lap. He opened them, and in his bandaged palm he saw his parents, working at the hospital and loving their newborn child enough to risk their own lives that he might grow up differently. Better. He felt something in his chest he wasn't sure he'd ever felt before. It hurt.

Then his thoughts returned to his prisoners.

"They'll publicly arrest you tomorrow, framing you all as perpetrators of a foiled assassination attempt. The news will work in the president's favor on Election Day, simultaneously demonstrating his strength and his mercy that he merely arrested and imprisoned you instead of having you executed."

"Aaren, your parents were killed in the Boycott Massacre a month after you were born. Militia overran the capital, and in their bloody sweep they stormed Central Hospital and rounded up as many government employees as they could find, including doctors, for public execution *in the name of the people*. They were likely unable to break into the heavily guarded officer nursery where you were lying helpless in a cradle. It was exactly the future your parents had feared."

Aaren absorbed this, then continued, "Joaquin, you and Han will likely be taken to a minimum-security facility in Epsilon. It's possible that in a few years you'll be eligible for parole."

Aaren turned to Natasha. "After the Election, you and Adler will surely be exiled." He didn't have to say it, but they knew—with the violence beyond the borders exile meant death.

"If the president is reelected, dissolving Congress will be only the beginning—"

"It doesn't matter. Nothing can change that now."

"You can change it—"

"No, I can't." Aaren raised his voice to make his point. "And even if I could, I wouldn't. Haline needs President Jemmer to lead us. There's no one else who could possibly take his place. It is what it is."

"It is what we make it."

"It's over, Natasha." Aaren stared at his prized prisoner. Even though he had only been tasked with dulling her voice, blocking her efforts, and otherwise containing the Cotter movement for a few months, he had originally felt honored by the assignment given the influence the Cotters had once had.

In those months, while he'd never succeeded in arresting Natasha, it was never ordered as a priority; "containment, not capture," his chief had said. In a way it had been a game of chess, and now his opponent sat across from him pathetic and vanquished. He supposed he should have felt a sense of victory or relief, but instead he was plagued by a growing sense of unease and doubt.

A buzz at the door roused Aaren from his thoughts. "One minute," he replied loudly, then walked to grab his transceiver and while replacing it over his ear moved to switch the camera back on and then open the slide door.

"We're ready to move them to Bunker One." The CG guard at the door eyed the room over Aaren's shoulder, curious what had gone on without surveillance.

"All right, move 'em."

15

ELECTION DAY—2 HOURS, 58 MINUTES BEFORE VOTING BEGINS
0402 HOURS, BETA RING

Aaren couldn't sleep that night. The identity and life he had worked so incredibly hard to build for himself brick by brick had been rocked as if by a mighty earthquake. By four in the morning he gave up even trying to sleep, and with nowhere else to go he found himself in his transport heading to Bunker One to see Natasha. Yes, she had started the earthquake—but then perhaps she also knew a way to stop it. Her fight was over so she would have no ulterior motive; hopefully, she would still be kind enough to help him understand.

Aaren walked up the steps of Bunker One, then through gate security with a wave of his wrist above the scanner. He took the short walk through the bodyscreen, then into the building and down the side stairs to the CG wing. He had never liked the president's Citizen Guard; they never treated him with the respect he believed he'd earned. As he approached the office he feared this meant they weren't treating Natasha with the respect that he felt she deserved, despite her situation.

"I'm here to see the Cotter prisoners." He walked up to the fortified window separating the CG wing from the rest of the bunker and spoke to the on-duty Guard soldier, flashing his wrist above the scanner. A monotone "Lieutenant Aaren Jemmer, clearance accepted" was SAI's soft reply, and Aaren moved to walk through the opening slide door when an arm reached out and held him where he stood.

"You're not authorized."

"What? You heard SAI, clearance accepted. Stand down and step aside." Though technically his rank was superior to the soldier, he knew he was pushing it. The Citizen Guard always had their orders direct from the president. But he was on a mission.

"The president has commanded no visitors for the Cotter prisoners. Your admittance is not allowed."

"He's what? I'm the one who—"

"Lieutenant Jemmer. Is there a problem?"

The voice caused every muscle in Aaren to tense, and he saw in the now-saluting CG soldier what he turned to see for himself.

"Mr. President, good morning! I hope they didn't call you? I'm incredibly, incredibly sorry if they did...it's so early!"

"No, no, not at all...it's a big day, Lieutenant. Assured in my victory as I might be, I always find it difficult to sleep the night before an Election. I suppose it's the thrill of millions of voices coming together as one, demanding one single thing, peacefully and powerfully."

"I can understand that, sir."

"Indeed. And you? What brings you here so early, Aaren?"

"I, uh, wished to pay my respects to Natasha, sir. I imagine you'll be exiling her today or tomorrow, and given that I spent much of the last few months containing the Cotters and tracking her, I wanted to say goodbye."

The president gave Aaren a smile in reply, pulling his lips loosely over his teeth, his hands still clasped behind his back, eyes twinkling.

"That would have been fitting. You are correct in your presumption that I would exile them, but incorrect in your timing. They were transported beyond the Haline border just minutes ago. I sent them straight from Central Studio." The president looked closely at Aaren, analyzing his face for any reaction of discontent. He found nothing.

"I see. A wise decision, sir. Today is too important to take any risks."

"Ah, Lieutenant. You overestimate the Cotters. Curious that you do so after watching them for several months. They posed no risk. It was simply easier to move them in the dark of night than wait, as we'll all be busy today and over the next several weeks as the mandate of the Election is understood and processed by this government and its people."

The president unclasped his hands and brought them forward, holding the datacard out in his right palm.

"This, Aaren, this was the only risk, and you recovered it for me. For that, I will be forever grateful." The president put the datacard on the protruding shelf in front of the CG window, withdrew the small self-defense beam gun holstered around his right thigh, and at close range incinerated it. It sparked and smoked into oblivion. Replacing the gun, he smiled again—this time, baring all his teeth. He was genuinely elated.

Aaren was surprised to feel a sense of loss as the card smoldered. He still had no idea what its contents had been, but clearly they had been incredibly important and so perhaps deserved to be preserved. As if reading his thoughts the president asked, "You never saw the media on the card, did you, Aaren?"

"No. No sir, not at all. It was never in my possession even if I had wanted to." The president saw the authenticity he was looking for, and the remaining bit of tension that sat on his shoulders melted away.

"Good. It wasn't anything truly worrisome of course, but even the smallest, most harmless kernel of truth can be twisted into the largest, most grotesque lie. And that's what we had to avoid."

"Of course, sir."

"Of course." The president reclasped his hands behind his back and looked upon the shorter, stockier Aaren a moment longer.

"You're a hero, Aaren, and you will be recognized accordingly once things calm down after the Election. For now, go on home and relax. Get out to the Zeta Ring and celebrate a bit. You've earned some time off."

"Thank you, sir. I might. I appreciate the kind words, sir."

The president turned to take his leave, and Aaren snapped to attention. As Aaren relaxed, the president, a few steps farther away now, turned back around. "Oh, one more thing. Before you go, be sure and vote, will you? I'm secretly hoping to lock in fifty percent of the electorate by noon."

"Of course, sir!" Aaren snapped back to attention and waited for the president to walk out of the room before relaxing. He offered the CG soldier that had watched the whole exchange a contemptuous glance and then turned and walked out the way he had come in, not sure where it was he was going.

**

Natasha awoke to a pounding headache, dry lips, sore limbs, and nausea. She opened her eyes to blackness, and feeling her eyelashes brush against a cloth, she realized she was blindfolded. Afraid to move, Natasha focused her hearing on the soft hum of an idling transport. After a moment she dared movement, pressing her knee and feeling the subtlest give. *Bare ground?*

"That's it. Let's go."

The voice had resentment about it, and it disappeared into the growing roar of the transport's engines. Wind pushed against her face, and she instinctively tried to turn her body, feeling for the first time that she was nearly on top of someone else.

The transport's engines faded into the distance and Natasha ventured a guess: "Adler?"

A groan was the reply, followed by, "Natasha…you all right? Yeah, it's me…but I feel a wreck."

"Yeah, me too. You blindfolded? Hands cuffed?"

A pause, and then "Afraid so."

"Hey guys, glad to hear you up." The voice was Joaquin's.

"Joaquin, is that you? My God, I can't believe they exiled you with us! You don't deserve this…I was certain they would have spared you our fate, for appearances if for nothing else…"

"It's fine, Natasha…I chose this path. Han is the one I'm sorry about. He had no idea what he was getting into, and I'm pretty sure he's here too…Han! You here?"

"Ah! What? Where am I? I can't see!"

"Han! It's me, Joaquin. Calm down…you're blindfolded. And you were snoring peacefully like you were on some damn vacation so I figured it was time to welcome you to your reality. Sucks, don't it."

"Ahhh…shit. I was having the best dream, Joaquin. You should have seen her."

"Natasha's here, Han."

"Oh! Uh…sorry, Natasha. Err…Ma'am."

Despite her condition Natasha couldn't help but chuckle, and she swore she heard Adler give a giggle.

"No apology necessary, Han…I needed that. I don't think I've smiled once the past twenty-four hours. Can everyone sit up okay? Any broken bones?"

"Okay here." Han replied.

"Here too, Natasha." Joaquin chimed in. "I actually woke up while we were still in transit—they drugged us you know—and overheard a bit of their conversation when they stopped to drop us off."

"Any idea where we are?" There was the tiniest bit of hope in Natasha's voice.

"I know exactly where we are and I think you do too." Joaquin's reply was definitive.

Natasha paused, and then somberly voiced the fear she knew to be the truth. "Beyond the wall, probably Delta gate."

"That's right."

"Aaren warned us they'd drop us off beyond the wall, but the Delta gate…" Adler's voice drifted off.

"They added an extra hour to their journey just to make a point." Natasha wanted to growl or scream in frustration but the others looked to her to lead their way. She could betray no such emotion, so she buried it next to the growing pile of anger at the bottom of her chest.

"What's so big about the Delta gate?" Han didn't bother biting his tongue anymore. He was beyond that point. They were all beyond that point.

"It's the gate that opens up to the mountains. Nothing around for miles and miles...just...the mountains." Adler's exhausted tone matched everyone's mood. "And it's the gate closest to Latmero."

"Oh." Han was sorry he asked.

"Yeah. Well. At least we're all in one piece." Natasha let out a long sigh.

"I'm sorry, Natasha. I wish...yeah, I just...I'm sorry."

"None of this is your fault, Adler, and if we're going to survive the day we have to let go of Haline, the Election, everything and focus on our current situation. Can you do that?"

"Yes, Natasha, I just don't see—"

"That's because you have a blindfold on. Just thank your God that our feet aren't bound. At least we can move. Adler, give me a low hum so I can get to exactly where you are. I'm going to try to take your blindfold off."

Adler started a hum as Natasha, on her knees, moved even closer to him. Getting behind him, she bent her face toward the back of his head and made contact with the cloth. Exposing her teeth, she pulled at the knot until it gave.

As the blindfold came off Adler, he blinked to make sure he was seeing what he thought he saw: a night sky kissed with a dawning light out into the distance.

"Adler, you good? See anything? First thing we need is cover...we'll burn out here without sun shield. Is it out yet? I don't feel it."

Adler swung his gaze around, and as he did he wished he could snap his eyes back shut.

"Adler?"

"Natasha..." Adler's quiet voice betrayed the fear he fought to control.

"What...what is it?" Han had been infected by Adler's tone.

Adler saw that he didn't have to say anything; in a few seconds, his companions could see for themselves. As each of their blindfolds came off they embraced a reality they thought they had just left: they were prisoners.

part three

16

ELECTION DAY—1 HOUR AND 59 MINUTES BEFORE VOTING BEGINS
0501 HOURS, OUTSIDE HALINE DELTA GATE

"What makes you four special enough to get dropped off by Citizen Guard soldiers outside Delta gate?" The man with the question spoke with the casual comfort of someone in obvious command. And given the situation—an entourage of eight armed soldiers, four of whom had standard Haline-issue officer-class minmax guns pointed directly at Natasha, Adler, Joaquin, and Han—he was quite confident of his place in the hierarchy.

"Who are you?" The question left Joaquin's lips before he knew he'd asked it. What began as a simple decision to investigate historical frames on a datacard, the past forty-eight hours had turned into something much bigger than just satisfying a curiosity. It was changing everything about the way Joaquin viewed the world, and himself.

"Judging by your handcuffs and the timing of your exile mere hours before the start of the Haline Election, I'm going to assume you are Cotters who attempted to execute a disruption scheme of some kind. You." He shined a light at Natasha, causing her to squint and turn her head. "You wear the close-cropped hair of Natasha and might even be her, though you look a bit younger than we've been led to believe. That would make you Adler by your height and clothing." The flashlight moved. Same reaction.

"And you two are the men Haline Police had been conducting a statewide sweep for. Your photos were transmitted to every Haline officer with the warning 'extremely dangerous,' though at the moment you both look quite harmless."

"Who are you?" Joaquin repeated his question with a flat tone, as if silence had greeted him the first time.

The man stared at Joaquin with an intensity equal to the flashlight, then shifted his gaze to Natasha, then Adler, then Han. Then he looked up at the soldier directly across from him, who stood behind Natasha. The soldier met the man's eyes with a slight nod, and the man offered a nod in return.

"The real answer requires a lengthy explanation that we don't have time for, but the short answer is we are your friends. One of our sentries spied the Delta gate open and sounded the alarm. Once we realized it was an exile and not an attack, we had our guesses as to who it might be. Matthias, let's get their cuffs off...we need to clear out of here quickly."

**

A forty-minute modified-transport ride later, they were miles from the walls of Haline at the base of a mighty mountain range that rose steep into the predawn sky. Their cuffs had been removed, but they had been separated for transport, each paired with a member of their new group of "friends."

There wasn't much to see as the landscape changed from a barren desert-like wasteland to rolling dead hills supporting only weed and bush growth. As those hills climbed, their path curved until they reached a mountain wall; here they parked their camouflaged transports, brought Natasha, Adler, Joaquin, and Han back together, then formed a single-file line and began on foot into a mountain pass.

A mere five minutes into their silent walk, the man turned and lifted a gun back in their direction and, within seconds, they were surrounded again by eight soldiers at gunpoint.

"Who are you?" The man with the original question offered a simpler one.

"What? You know who we are...we didn't even have to say anything. Who are *you* to have all this Haline-standard equipment outside of Haline?" Natasha's mind had been racing, exploring all options around who her new friends were while also contemplating scenarios that would allow her back into Haline in time. She barely heard the question in her mental trance but knew it was directed at her.

"That's who we believed you to be, but that doesn't explain why a Haline transport—a speeder, no less—was just spotted coming through Delta gate and is heading in this direction. If it gets within a half mile of our present location we will bring it down, which will raise alarms back at Haline. This we can't afford. So I'll ask again—who are you?"

"Aaren!" Natasha was overcome with a joy she hadn't felt in ages.

"Who is Aaren?"

"Aaren is...never mind, it would take too long to explain. The short answer is he's a friend...I think. How far away is he?" Natasha's mind was racing again with possibility.

"Only about ten minutes...as I said, he's on a speeder. Four times faster than officer-class transports." The man was skeptical, but cooperative. "He must be important, unless he stole it."

"He didn't steal it. Can I intercept him without exposing you? So you don't have to bring him down." Natasha took a step forward and was poised to run in any direction the man pointed in.

"Yes but..." The man pondered the alterative—bringing the speeder down—and the worst-case scenario of this being some kind of Election Day ambush. He wouldn't put it past the president but...Natasha seemed to be the Natasha he'd heard about.

"You'll have to hurry. Take that path there, up to that

ledge. You see it? His scanner should pick up your movement and alter his course. His angle of approach should then keep us hidden from view. Go quickly!"

In a quiet voice she hoped only her team could hear Natasha whispered: "Guys, stay here. I'm near positive it's Aaren…I think he's come around."

"Too little too late, right?" Adler was skeptical.

"Maybe not. Let's hope I'm right." Natasha bolted for the ledge and left her team behind with their new friends.

"Can you lower your guns please? I assure you we are who you think we are." Having been shot and wounded a handful of times, Adler loathed guns pointed in his direction. The morning excitement in the outdoor, ozone-saturated air strained his lungs, and he pulled out his balancer and inhaled.

"Adler, if that's who you are, we haven't survived out here this long without being ambushed by your government by assuming people always tell the truth. But it looks like we have some time, so convince me. Answer my original question. How is it that you ended up getting dropped off outside Delta gate on Election Day?"

"Well, I suppose it's Joaquin's story to tell, as it sort of began with him. Joaquin, how did you come across that datacard?"

Joaquin let out a long sigh and then ventured a smile and recounted the last forty-eight hours of his life.

President Jemmer leaned forward in his chair with the calm hint of a smile. His eyes moved between screens, one displaying constantly updating voter polls by Ring as canvassed by his Election staff and calculated by SAI, and the other the morning news. He was expected in the war room once voting began, but he had these few minutes to discreetly savor his pending victory, as well as the one he had managed just hours ago.

A thought struck him, flattening his lips, and he popped open his hidden comm drawer and pulled out his secure screen. His message regarding the destruction of the datacard had gone unanswered, and he was anxious to connect with her before his day—his big day—began. His patience exhausted, he opened a channel. She would not ignore the request.

"What is it, Gaven."

"Venka." It was all he could reply with. The rare times when he opened up a channel it was always the same thing—a feeling of fear mixed with awe at the sight of her.

Venka sought him out when Gaven began his ascent through the military ranks. Over time, she won his confidence and then guided him to continued victories and more power, then to control over all of Haline, and then through the first Election—and every day since. As those days passed, his relationship with Venka moved from a friendship of allies with a shared desire and destiny to a hierarchy of master and servant. And he was the servant.

"We got your message."

"Great. I wanted to confirm you knew things were going according to plan on this end. My staff is—"

"You forget I see what you're seeing, and more, Gaven. I know exactly what's being predicted. All that aside, the events of the past twenty-four hours have ruffled feathers. The Board is considering its options."

"The Board!" Gaven Jemmer fought to control his surprise. "Venka, I assure you everything is going as requested. As you said, you can see that yourself."

"Yes, but it's not that simple. I can't explain now, but a word of advice—watch the Delta gate. It appears your Lieutenant Aaren Jemmer is attempting some sort of rescue mission of the exiles."

"What? SAI hasn't notified me…" His eyes moved to SAI's priority screen on the left wall. It was blank.

"Aaren has Alpha 2–class security clearance. Out of SAI's domain. Just be vigilant. I'll reconnect with you later this morning when we have some numbers."

The screen flashed black, leaving Gaven to see the outlines of his own face reflected back at him off the shine from its surface. His wide eyes and furrowed brow betrayed more than he wanted to.

17

Natasha emerged down the path followed closely by Aaren. She was happy to see that their new friends were no longer pointing their weapons at her comrades and couldn't help but smile; perhaps she would survive the day after all.

Or maybe not. Natasha's smile vanished as guns were pointed at Aaren with the words "Stay right there!"

"He's not an officer. Not anymore, anyway."

"Officers are born officers, Natasha. You know that."

"That's just the thing. He *wasn't* born an officer. His parents worked at Central Hospital and were Cotters. They smuggled him into the officer nursery at birth so he could have a better life."

The man with the question—Rylan, as Joaquin, Han, and Adler now knew—was the one who broke the uncomfortable silence that followed, his words apprehensive. "Impossible. He's lying to you, Natasha."

"He didn't know until yesterday, when we told him

based on our knowledge of who his parents were. He's lived his whole life as if he was in fact born an officer, afraid to tell anyone that he didn't believe he actually shared the genetically enhanced reflexes and strength and stamina of his peers."

Rylan exchanged glances of disbelief with Matthias, then turned back to Aaren—but spoke to Natasha: "Incredible...but, how can you be sure?"

Natasha spun a roundhouse kick to Aaren's solar plexus, knocking him down and leaving him breathless. He began coughing, and his face reddened as he looked up with questioning eyes and anger at Natasha.

"That was for shooting at me." Natasha spoke the words sternly down to Aaren as she stood above him, but a smile resurfaced on her face and she offered Aaren a hand up. "Even?"

Behind her, she had elicited the response she was looking for—the soldiers were all laughing and nodding, and guns were lowered. A true officer would not be so weak as to display the normal, expected reaction from a kick to the chest.

"An excellent answer, Natasha. Where did you learn to roundhouse like that?" The lines on Rylan's weathered face were not used to shaping into a smile, but they did what they could.

"When Julian recruited me to the Cotters I told them no guns, so they made me learn how to use my legs." Natasha smiled.

Rylan reached out a hand of his own. "My name is Rylan. I lead this band of brothers and sisters."

Natasha had turned back after helping Aaren to his feet and took Rylan's hand. Rylan brought his other hand to clasp hers. "We call ourselves Patriots. You might know us as Latmero fighters."

"What?! You are the Latmero fighters?" Again, Natasha's mind spun.

"Yes, we are. I know what lies they broadcast on your screens. We are made to look quite menacing, aren't we?"

"Yes, and…" Natasha's thoughts shifted gears from a trot to a gallop. "I don't understand…where is Latmero then? Or do you live here, in these mountains? We were told they were radioactive. Uninhabitable."

"Natasha, there is a lot you have been led to believe that is false. The truth is my troops and I are from what is now Haline and were on the other side of the battle when President Jemmer was clinching his power in the old capital. Once we saw defeat eminent, we fled."

Natasha turned to her companions and saw on each of their faces the same look of surprise as she was sure she wore. She took a breath and tried accepting what she was hearing as the truth—but when she did, a flood of questions came to her. "What do you eat? Where does your water come from? How do you protect yourself from the sun's radiation?"

"Again, Natasha, the notion that genetically engineered vegmos are the only produce that can grow in our schizophrenic environment is a farce. We initially shared your fears, but in these mountains discovered heirloom breeds that survived the worst—or you might say the best— of our engineering. Water, too, is not as scarce as you believe, and we have erected our own protective shield from the sun's rays."

Rylan paused, seeing in Natasha's now blank expression a need to slow down.

"It has not been easy, but we have survived in these mountains for seven years. Not food nor water nor radiation is our concern. Rather, it is being attacked by President Jemmer. As such we've kept a watchful eye on your Haline. The mild 'Latmero' incursions you have heard about have been us as we sought information and equipment to prepare for our inevitable war. Thus far, we've never sought confrontation or casualties."

Rylan walked a few paces toward Matthias and nodded, prompting him to pick up where Rylan left off: "Ironically, Natasha, part of our survival is due to flawed planning. See these two cracks in the rock?" He pointed.

"And the way they radiate out as a ridge into the foothills? They are the result of an earthquake some ten years ago caused by a rupture in a carbon sequestration unit buried beneath these mountains. Though the carbon leaked back into the atmosphere with the quake, fortunately for us the land shift exposed rich, protected soil with dormant seeds that we were able to farm."

Natasha, Han, Joaquin, Adler, and Aaren all remained silent and worked to comprehend what they were hearing. Matthias turned back to Rylan with a small shrug.

"Natasha, in time we will show you everything." Rylan interjected with a calm voice. "President Jemmer and the governments before him have all worked to create a false reality to blind the people from the truth. It will take time for this truth to be accepted and understood by you, as it did for us."

Rylan moved a step closer to Natasha. "For now, while I disagree with your nonviolent approach and am not surprised to see your movement failing, I must say you have nonetheless earned my respect for your work and your patience. It is truly an honor to meet you.

"Your friend Joaquin here..." Rylan walked the two steps to a still-quiet Joaquin, putting an arm around his shoulder, "has also earned our respect with his act of bravery in seeking to truly understand."

"He has earned our respect as well." Color returned to Natasha as she inhaled to focus and push the questions and doubts from her mind. "Rylan, sir, it is an honor to meet you. I can't believe you are the Latmero fighters that scary bedtime stories are made of."

She smiled, then tilted her head and looked down in thought a moment before looking up. "I have to ask. You say you've only been after information and equipment these years you've been in hiding. What do you do with it all? What's your plan?"

"To overthrow the president, of course. To bring down his false government and the framework of lies upon which it is built. Oh, the stories I could tell you and the things I could show you, you would scant believe. But come...the sun is about to rise and already the day has been rather eventful. Let's break our fast and share more about our two independent wars with this president and see how we might consolidate and collaborate." Rylan moved toward the mountain pass but was stopped by Natasha's hand on his shoulder.

"Rylan, with all due respect, we don't have time. As you yourself noted, today is Election Day. We can't let him get a third term. We have strong evidence that he intends to dissolve Congress."

"Does he?" This was news to Rylan, and he stopped cold to consider its implications. "Where did you get this information?"

"One of our contacts in Alpha who has always been reliable."

"Natasha, surely you understand the potential consequences—"

"Why do you think it's so important we return? Today?" Natasha took a step forward.

Rylan paused and prophesized a milder outcome:

"Perhaps it will serve our cause as those statesmen and women return to be with their people and spread seeds of discontent for the administration."

"Rylan, knowing the president, that is doubtful. He's surely thought through that contingency and will blackmail, bribe, or if he has to, imprison every single one of them to preserve the approval ratings he is so proud of. And without them in his way, he'll push through the full security agenda that so far Congress has kept at bay—and more."

"Indeed." Rylan reflected again for a moment. "That is incredibly frightening news, Natasha, but I still do not see what options we have. Especially today, with security on high alert and—given your friend's journey from Haline in a speeder, despite the fact that he's an authorized officer—the police chief's likely expanded monitoring around the Delta gate. Our best option is to regroup, wait for the Election to pass, and then evaluate. This can work in our favor if we use the disbanded congressional members as our allies on the inside."

"That will be too late!" Natasha caught the emotion in her throat, and closing her eyes, she took a deep breath to will it back down into place. "That will be too late. And we do have a plan. Joaquin," Natasha walked to him, "Aaren saw the datacard incinerated this morning by the president. I'm sorry. I know the very reason you began your journey was to understand its secrets."

Joaquin kept quiet a moment, overcome by a passing

sense of loss but quickly recovering and recognizing again his new reality. "It's fine, Natasha. The past forty-eight hours...it's about so much more than a datacard now."

His eyes lingered in hers a moment before he turned to Rylan. "Will you help us?"

"Commit suicide? I will not. We have waited this long for a reason. And I still have not heard of any plan."

Natasha answered quickly. "Aaren disabled his transceiver before beginning his journey, so neither SAI nor the Haline police are aware of his whereabouts, or the speeder's. We can easily reenter through Delta gate and make our way to a broadcast station and then hack a signal with footage of your testimonial."

"Testimonial! Expose ourselves? Absolutely not. We haven't waited this long only to be hunted like dogs just so you can kick up some dust in a fight you are fated to lose."

She continued, "Rylan, think of it. If the people heard from you that the Latmero fighters are a fabrication, if they knew of the existence of a people, *our* people, a mere one hundred miles outside Haline city limits—"

"Out of the question! And besides, no one would believe it."

Natasha's eyes flashed desperation and then signaled acquiescence. She lowered her head a moment then raised her eyes to meet his. "Well then we part ways. I cannot sit idly by while this Election unfolds to empower him to do more harm than he's already done."

"What. Is. Your. Plan." Rylan leaned in and spoke not with anger, but resolve.

"I don't have one yet." Natasha matched his tone.

They stood there, eyes locked.

"Do not do this. You will not survive. Join us and we can march together when the time is right."

"The time is now."

"It most certainly is not! Consider the odds, Natasha. You are blinded by your desire to redeem yourself after years of waging a losing war. Well I have news. The war will not end today, or tomorrow, or next week. Your fight has been valiant but is part of a broader war being fought on many fronts. Together, we can and will vindicate your efforts, but today is *not* the day."

Natasha spoke with measured words. "We cannot win this fight without the people, and there is no better day than Election Day to reach and influence those people."

Rylan looked upon her and then moved his eyes to Adler, then to Joaquin, then to Han, then to Aaren—and then back to Natasha.

"Leave Joaquin and Han with us. They are mere civilians and need not perish under the chip that weighs upon your shoulder."

"We stand with Natasha." Again, Joaquin surprised himself. But he owned the words once they left his mouth. The thought of Han actually wanting to stay behind flashed into his mind, but he dismissed it. Han's loyalty outweighed his fear. He'd proven that much in the last two days.

"Well then...I wish you luck." Rylan turned to continue into the pass and his soldiers followed. A few steps on, however, Rylan motioned his troops forward, turned, and called out. "Natasha...a word."

Natasha gave Adler and then Joaquin a look, then walked to where Rylan had sat down on a rock and joined him.

"Natasha. I am sorry if my comments were harsh but I know what you fight for, and want to help you win your fight."

"I understand Rylan...no offense taken."

"You know, for a second back there I thought I was arguing with myself." He surrendered a brief smile. "You are perhaps as stubborn as the aging man who sits beside you on this rock. Surely not more so."

Natasha smiled. "I assume that means there is no way to convince you to join us."

"None, Natasha, I am sorry."

"I understand."

"I meant it when I said it was an honor to meet you, you know. I actually met your parents once, before you were born, during the wars—though I knew your mother by reputation for many years. Wonderful people, incredibly strong. Justice was their compass." He turned and put his hand on Natasha's shoulder. "You make them proud."

Natasha felt her heart sadden, then flutter. Was there a

higher compliment she could ever be paid? "Thank you."

"There is more to the story than the president, Natasha. It may surprise you to hear it, but he is in fact powerless before his superiors—yes, superiors." He answered Natasha's jolted face.

"Wha…" Natasha shook her head to clear it. "Rylan, what superiors? What are you talking about?"

"Natasha, I dare not explain any further as, and forgive me for saying this, I don't want the depth of our knowledge to be exposed under the torture I fear you will be subjected to if you are captured. Just know that I believe the president is doing and will continue to do what he feels he must in order to preserve his peace, and so his place, which makes him…unpredictable."

"Rylan, tell me. What superiors? Who?" Natasha's curiosity burned, but as she stared at his stone face she realized pursuing the topic would be a waste of time. "Fine. I have no idea what you're talking about, but I'll keep it in mind."

"Do that. You know, Gaven and I were friends once…close friends, in fact." He turned his eyes from the side of the cliff ahead of him to acknowledge the renewed look of shock on Natasha's face.

"It helps me sleep at night to believe that he does what he does because he has no choice."

"How? I don't under—"

"We fought together in the wars, back when it was

more obvious who the enemy was. I was his superior officer, in fact, and though I may have been a few years older I was just as ambitious as he was back then." Rylan looked at Natasha and saw in her a patient, eager audience. He continued.

"We had our different reasons, but we both believed that the path to stability was in the consolidation of power. Together and with select others from our ranks, we aligned ourselves with the party we believed had both the best intentions and the best odds at emerging victorious. We succeeded, but those were terrible, terrible days, the horrors of which I pray we never see again."

"What happened?"

"Hmm? Oh, you mean how did Gaven and I end up on opposing sides. Venka, that's how." He paused, his face dark. "She came from great wealth and greater power, and seeing something in Gaven, she wooed him to a splinter faction that, over the course of the following year, worked to depose our original party leadership. The next thing I knew, Gaven was party leader and I was declared an enemy of the state along with the rest of those who remained loyal to the ousted government."

He paused and hopped off the rock on which he had been sitting. "It's a long story, Natasha, but the short of it is Gaven and his soldiers continued to consolidate power. Some of us kept fighting, but as soon as we realized we were only days away from capture or worse, we fled for these mountains."

He paused again, looking toward Haline. "I'm certain Gaven knows we are here, and I believe it is the remnants of our friendship that attract his blind eye." Natasha remained silent, wanting more. Rylan continued.

"Natasha, Gaven does not lead Haline, and your fight against him today will accomplish little, even at the improbable chance that you do succeed."

Few words came to her, and she stared into her thoughts and shook her head. "I...I don't understand..."

"With what little you know, you can't understand, young Natasha. You are not ready for your fight. But morning is upon us, so if you truly intend to take action today you must get on your way quickly. If at any point you change your mind, flee to the Delta gate and we will do what we can to protect you."

"I do and I will. Thank you, Rylan. For everything."

"I only wish I could talk you out of this. Then I might deserve that thanks, some days or weeks or months from now when you would realize the futile nature of your ambition. But I can't...so I wish you strength and success."

Natasha embraced Rylan as she might have her father, holding him with the love of years though it had not been an hour. Rylan's eyes moistened as they separated, and he caught Natasha's hand as she turned to go.

"Wait." Rylan paused. "Natasha, there is something I should tell you...that you should know before you return.

That perhaps will convince you *not* to return."

Natasha stopped and met his eyes.

Rylan looked past Natasha to make sure they were well out of earshot from her companions. "You will find this immensely troubling but...you deserve to know. Especially today as you go in for perhaps your last battle against him, though I hope it will convince you not to."

"What is it, Rylan?" Natasha locked her eyes with his as Rylan took her hands into his own and clasped them tightly.

Rylan opened his mouth, closed his mouth, and then looked down before he could continue. "Natasha, tell me, how clearly do you remember your youth? Your family, specifically?"

Caught off guard by the question, it took Natasha a moment to reply. Shaking her head, "I think I remember a lot. My mother and father were everything to me. They were very brave, both of them...even as a child I was very proud of them. Protective, even."

"And?"

"And what?"

"And any siblings?"

"I—yes. I had an older brother, but...I remember very little about him. He was eleven years older than me. I was barely two when he left home, never to return. Mom and dad never spoke of him after that. The few times I brought it up, they told me he had been 'lost to the wars' as so many others had been. It made them so emotional I never pushed further." She paused, remembering. "Rylan, why are you—"

"His name, do you remember his name?"

"I...no, come to think of it, I don't." Natasha's eyes closed as she worked to recall it. She began feeling nauseous. "My parents...I think they called him..."

"Vee."

"Yes, yes! Vee, that's right." She opened her eyes as a curious look shaped her face. "Rylan, how did you—"

"Natasha, think back to him. Remember him. What do you see?"

Natasha tried closing her eyes again, but opened them after a brief moment. "Rylan, I'm feeling dizzy. I have to get back—"

"Natasha." He paused. "Gaven Jemmer...is Vee, your brother."

"What...what are you talking about?" Her voice sharpened.

"He's your brother, Natasha. I know because that's when I first met him, with your parents before you were born. We were in school together, your brother and I."

"I don't understand..." As his words sank in, hers barely got out.

"I don't know how to tell you this, but I believe they altered your memory, Natasha. It was another system of control, placing you to lead the Cotters and him to lead Haline."

Fear gripped Natasha's face.

"Natasha, your brother left home for boarding school at thirteen. But he came home again at seventeen for months before being deployed and visited often after that. Do you remember?"

He felt her grip weaken and held her hands tighter, moving his piercing gaze from her left eye to her right and back, working to keep her present.

"I…" Natasha's nightmare returned to her and she closed her eyes, feeling bound at her wrists and ankles. She shook her head and opened her eyes. "Rylan, what are you talking about…*who altered my memory?*"

"I told you, Natasha, this is much bigger than President Jemmer, much bigger than Haline. I cannot tell you, and even if I did you wouldn't believe me, just as you don't believe me now." Rylan saw the look of initial fear on Natasha's face giving way to anger. He pressed on.

"But listen, you have time…with Aaren's speeder, you can get there and back in half an hour and see with your own eyes what I can never describe."

Natasha's eyes glazed as she lost herself in her head, her nightmare coming back…altered her memory…the president was her brother…*no, it isn't true*.

"You're lying. You're lying to me, Rylan…why would you lie? Who are you to do this?" She yanked her hands out of his and took a step back.

"Here, take this datacard." He reached into his pocket and retrieved the tiny device. "Nothing I say will convince you of the truth, so go see it with your own eyes. Follow the flight plan on the card exactly, do you understand? It's absolutely critical you don't deviate an inch. When you're ready to return and begin your journey back to Haline, retrace your steps here first. While I pray that what you see will convince you to stay here with us, even if you choose to return to Haline I'll know you are safely on your way home when my sentry reports your speeder. Now go."

Natasha absentmindedly held the datacard and stared at Rylan a moment, searching for some motive for him to deceive her. She found none, and her mind went back to the memory of her and Ashten at the ocean...or, as she was cautiously, reluctantly beginning to accept, her and Gaven Jemmer.

"I should get back to Haline...I don't have time for this." Natasha pushed the datacard back in Rylan's direction, but he closed his hands around hers and pushed it back toward her.

"Natasha, the secret to understanding your fight back in Haline is here, in the coordinates on this card." Rylan let go of Natasha's hands. "And if you understand your fight, you'll be better prepared to succeed. I promise you that."

Still in a daze, Natasha looked at Rylan a second longer then turned to rejoin her comrades, working to clear her head with a few deep breaths on the way. They had brought the speeder and were finishing a breakfast provided by Rylan's team. She noticed Joaquin and Han now both had officer-class minmax guns holstered around their thighs.

Seeing her approach, Han asked the question on everyone's mind: "So, what's the plan?"

"I'm not sure, but we don't have time to waste figuring one out. Let's go."

18

As the speeder door closed, Natasha looked out the window back at the pass that Rylan and his soldiers had disappeared through and shook her head. "Damn him." Her sad tone mismatched her words.

Turning around, she closed her eyes, took a deep breath, then exhaled with a question: "Do you guys mind if we take a quick detour? There's something Rylan wants us to see. Something…that might somehow help us today."

"It's up to you, Natasha." Joaquin spoke for all of them. In Natasha they trusted.

"Aaren." Natasha got up, reached into her pocket—she disobeyed the Haline laws she disagreed with—and pulled out the datacard Rylan had given her. "There's a hyper-specific flight plan on this card. Can you access it?"

Aaren took the card, touched the pad to activate it, and placed it on the console. Immediately the windshield had a map of their destination—ETA, sixteen minutes at top speed.

"We have no idea what we're going to find?" Aaren asked. Natasha was not his leader.

"None."

He turned in his chair to Natasha, who stood with her head bent and her right hand on his shoulder, and gave her an "I don't think this is a good idea" look.

"Please." Natasha's desire to see what Rylan was talking about grew with each passing minute. Partially because of what she still didn't believe about her brother. But mostly because whatever was there clearly bothered Rylan, and that bothered her.

"All right, buckle up." Aaren turned back to the console and, punching a few buttons, lifted the speeder off the ground. Natasha returned to her seat and strapped in.

"Well, we've got about sixteen minutes before, according to Rylan, we see something...I don't know. Whatever it is, let's be productive in the meantime. Anyone got any ideas for once we get back to Haline?"

Adler was first to reply. "We do have one advantage: Aaren's speeder, and of course Aaren himself. What if he went to the houses of key congressional members and arrested them? Word would get out, people would see it as entirely plausible that the president would power-grab, and—"

"Aaren won't help us. Not like that, anyway." Natasha looked up from the latch on the floor that had held her gaze. "He's not one of us, not yet. The only reason he came after us was a feeling of burning guilt at being responsible for our deaths, or exile, which to him meant the same thing. I had a hard time convincing him to take us back to Haline and not leave us in the welcoming hands of Rylan and his people."

She paused and turned her head to the cockpit door which Aaren had closed as they accelerated, happy that he could still hear every word she said. Maybe overhearing their plans would convince him to help. "Next idea."

"Could Aaren get us close to Bunker One?" Joaquin sat up straight, his eyes twinkling with thought.

"Probably, assuming Aaren would be okay with being that close. Why?"

"Security near Bunker One is notoriously thin for being the president's home. Just two squadrons of CGs housed there. The president himself often affirms that Haline is not a police state, despite the fact that his residence is a nuclear bomb-proof, one-hundred-foot-deep bunker. Perhaps we can get close enough to stun him, and—"

"No violence." As the words left her mouth, Natasha immediately wondered if that too had been part of the memory alteration. *Why am I so averse to violence?*

"I didn't say kill, I said stun, and—"

"No. Violence." Natasha's eyes softened as she strove to speak to both Joaquin's mind and his heart. "It's not our way. Violence is what got us into this reality. It is not the way out. Next idea." She dared not share the real reason she couldn't possibly consider firing on Gaven Jemmer.

A silence fell on the group until Han broke it with quiet words. "I have an idea."

All eyes turned to Han and, giving Joaquin a half smile, he continued. "Natasha, no one knows you. I mean *really* knows who you are and what you stand for. Given all that we've learned in the last forty-eight hours I can tell you the average Halinite would be shocked to hear a tenth of what you could tell them. I'm not sure why, but you've never spoken to them—to us—and explained *why* you do what you do."

He paused, looking back to Joaquin for support. "If you spoke to the people, even just for a minute, I think enough of them would listen to...to make a difference."

Natasha glanced at Adler, seeking approval. Getting a nod, she turned back to Han. "This movement was never about me, but about *you*, Haline's people, and about the president and his policies."

She paused. "While I tell myself that I've avoided the spotlight for safety reasons..." She returned her gaze back to the latch on the floor. "If it's our only option, I'll do it."

"Great. Now all we need to do is figure out how we'll broadcast. Joaquin, I assume—"

"You assume correctly, Han. After what they've already done to her, I want to leave Lyla completely out of this."

"Understood. To be honest, I figured hacking into a station was not an option, so I have another idea—a virus. Of sorts."

Eyebrows went up across the transport bay.

"Natasha, can I see you up here in the cockpit?" Aaren's voice came in sharp over the intercom.

"Just a minute, Aaren." Natasha spoke to the closed cockpit door then turned her head back to Han. "Continue."

"Transceivers are linked not only to SAI but can also be linked to each other if they are within a range of about one hundred feet. They were designed in this way as a redundancy mechanism should the core signal ever be compromised. If that happened, a device-to-device mesh network could carry messages between transceivers so long as they were within that hundred feet."

"Fascinating, but how do we turn this redundant network on if the core signal is still broadcasting? Unless you want us to try and—"

"No, no, that'd be futile, Alder. Activating the redundant network is a nontrivial hack that I happen to have done before. I just need a screen from which I can patch into a transceiver and trigger a falsified 'signal down' alarm. Once I do that it will automatically hop to any transceiver within range—in other words, spread like a virus."

"Where does the broadcast come in?"

"We can attach media to the trigger, which becomes a carrier of sorts. This is exactly what the redundancy was designed for."

"Natasha, I need you up here now." Aaren's voice boomed through the cabin.

Ignoring him, Natasha continued to Han, "If this were to work, we'd need a crowded area, correct? To be most effective?"

"That's right."

"Great. And I assume the moment you commit the hack, SAI will connect into Central and it'd be minutes before there were officers and scouts at your location."

"Or seconds, if they happen to be close by."

"Okay. I'll be right back." Unfastening her harness with a smile of hope on her face, Natasha pushed a button and the cockpit door slid open. Immediately, she realized why Aaren's voice had edges of concern.

"Where are we?" As Natasha uttered the words the speeder took a sharp left, throwing Natasha off balance. She grabbed Aaren's chair as he pushed a button; another chair emerged from the floor, and Natasha sat down in it, her mouth still gaping, her hands fastening the harness.

"Natasha, where are we going?"

"Aaren, I told you. I don't know."

"The card has locked me out of ship controls. Did you know that was going to happen?"

"He told me nothing of the sort. In fact, he gave me the impression that we'd have explicit flight-path control." She shook her head. "He knew I'd never agree to *this*."

"Guys, keep your seatbelts on...we're about five minutes away, but it's gonna be a dizzying five minutes." Aaren raised his voice as he spoke through the still-open cockpit door.

The ship took another sharp left and then dropped fifty feet, and the glimpses that Aaren and Natasha saw of their destination turned into darkness. They were in some sort of tunnel now, the ship automatically navigating its crevices in accordance with the flight path outlined in the datacard.

"You sure Rylan isn't trying to kill us?"

"If that was his intention he would have done that back at camp. And kept the speeder."

"Fair point." The logic was sound, but as the speeder pitched left, then right, then down, then up, Aaren wasn't wholly convinced.

"What are those flashing red lights on the map?" Natasha pointed at the windshield.

"I've been wondering the same thing." He turned to her. "I think they are mines. It would explain the zigs and zags."

A feeling of helplessness overcame Natasha. She closed her eyes to breathe, and the ship coursed through another minute of turns and drops and climbs before emerging into the soft light of dawn.

"We're through." Aaren turned to Natasha with a nervous smile.

"I still can't see anything."

"We're in some sort of a forest on the other side of the mountain, I think. The sun hasn't risen over the ridge yet. One minute to destin...a...tion." Aaren's voice crumbled to a whisper as they saw it spread out ahead of them in glimpses between the trees. The speeder decelerated, and Aaren's head whipped in Natasha's direction. Her face had whitened.

"That isn't…" Natasha couldn't finish the question, as the implication of the answer was more than she was ready to handle.

Unbuckling himself from his seat, Aaren pushed the button to open the speeder door while the craft slowed; an error ding was all he got. He turned back to the console once the craft had stopped seconds later and pushed the button again. He got the same reply.

The windshield darkened and the map gave way to Rylan's face. By this time Adler, Joaquin, and Han were standing at the open cockpit door and peering in to see what was going on.

> *If you're seeing this, then you've been authorized to understand what it is we're really fighting for. For your safety and ours, however, your transport doors will not open and you will only be at this location for ninety seconds before your transport begins its return journey, so pay close attention.*

Natasha turned to Adler, and they exchanged a look of intense confusion. The top right three quadrants of the windshield lightened, and Rylan's face and the map moved to the bottom left quadrant.

> *What stretches out below you is one of five*

city-states named Haline, each numbering roughly six million in population. Most likely you are from the Haline where the president is Gaven Jemmer, and most likely you believe you are the only Haline, surrounded by hostile countries that seek to destroy you—with one benevolent supplier partner. That is a false truth your president and his superiors have used to incite fear and create dependence.

All eyes were fixed on the sprawling metropolis beneath them, a curved wall running the circumference of the entire city-state, a series of more or less evenly spaced concentric circles dividing the land into distinct rings.

Each Haline has its own president and Congress to provide the illusion of self-governance, and each is structured in more or less the same way, with six distinct rings of class-stratified population. Technologies and laws are also mostly identical across each Haline.

Most critically, the source of supplies—food, water, energy—is identical, as they are all connected to a central production hub, a place known as the 'Supply Partner' to Halinites but that we believe is called Enve.

The screen morphed into an image of a sprawling, blinking city the likes of which no one there had ever seen.

While we know little of Enve, we know her power reaches back centuries and ultimately stems from her monopoly over raw materials and basic resources.

The images shifted to a map of five Halines clearly defined by circular walls, various distances from but distinctly around the center city of Enve.

> *At some point early in the wars, several entities aligned into a superentity of sorts, and over the course of a few years isolated each city-state. Enve then selected someone in each Haline to bring into power, first through battle, then through Elections. Each president submits to the authority of an Enve body known as* The Board.

The screen lightened again to reveal the metropolis beneath.

> *Each Haline exists solely as a market for Enve, which controls all production and all prices. Each Haline government exists solely to serve* The Board *at Enve. This is all we know, and it has taken years to find out the little information we have.*

The windshield darkened and Rylan's image overtook the field of view.

> *You have been entrusted with this information because we believe you can help. I'm sure you have questions.*

The speeder's engines began a quiet hum as they restarted.

*Upon your return we will answer what we
can.*

As the speeder lifted off the ground everyone numbly
returned to their seats in the main cabin and strapped in,
anticipating the nauseating ride back. Each mind struggled to
comprehend what it had just seen—leaving each mouth
empty of words.

"Natasha." Adler finally broke the silence with a
whimper of a whisper.

Natasha shook her head briskly and inhaled sharply. *The
president is my brother. And he works for…The Board? Haline
is…what? What is Enve? And Rylan. What is his part in all
this?* She struggled to organize her myriad of questions and
emotions into a cohesive thought.

Getting nothing from his superior, Adler looked down at
the floor and allowed himself to get lost in his own cerebral
maze. Meanwhile, Joaquin's mind was on his uncle. *Did he
know? He must have known…he tried to warn me.*

For a moment, Han tried to process everything—but all
he kept coming back to was an incredible, deep fear, so after
they were back above ground he unstrapped himself and
moved to the front of the craft to sit with Aaren and be
distracted by the terrain as they made their journey back.

Aaren stared blankly out the windshield. *Impossible. It
must have been a forged simulation. That's why they didn't
let us out.* He took a deep breath as he attempted to own his

conclusion as a truth, but his subconscious wasn't convinced. *So that's why the Citizen Guard answers only to the president...*

19

As they approached the starting point of their journey, where they had left Rylan and his soldiers, Natasha briefly considered stopping to get the answers Rylan had promised—but over the past sixteen minutes so many questions had flooded her head that she realized she might be here for weeks.

The speeder landed exactly where it had left and the datacard shut itself off, powering down the speeder's engines. Aaren immediately hit the button to power them back on and then turned to Natasha in the back.

"Where to?"

Natasha was staring at the floor. She inhaled, then lifted her head and looked around at her team. "Open the bay door."

The bay door slid open and Natasha stared out it a moment before continuing. "I...don't know what to tell you about what we just saw. I'm not sure of anything myself and know no more than you do. If true…I…I don't know what it all means, us being one of five, and…"

She paused. "Look, all I know for certain is this: the Haline that I know and have known my whole life is about to slip out of our reach, and I'm not going to let that happen." Natasha sat up straight in her seat as she found her strength.

"You each have the option to get off here and join Rylan, perhaps to fight another day, perhaps never to have to fight again. Even you, Adler." She looked with admiration upon her trusted companion of the past five years of struggle, then turned to the civilians.

"Joaquin, Han, twenty-four hours ago I would have pushed you out that door at gunpoint and left you here for your own safety—but you've both earned my highest respect so I'll instead ask you, please stay behind. This is not your fight."

"It is now, Natasha. After what they did to Lyla…it is now."

Natasha noticed that Joaquin had gained a calm intensity since their adventures began and realized there was no convincing him to stay.

"Uh…" Han, sitting up front, looked back at Natasha and then turned to Joaquin. "Can I have a word?"

"Yeah, sure." Joaquin looked at Natasha. "Since I don't trust you to not leave us here if we step out, I'm going to ask you to please give us a few minutes?"

Natasha smiled. "Your mistrust is well placed. Yeah,

we'll be outside." Natasha, Adler, and Aaren stepped out into the early morning, stretching and preparing for the long day ahead, none daring conversation about what they had just seen. They tried falling into their morning routines, each of them taking their daily anti-spore dose, Adler pulling breath from his ozone balancer to normalize his lungs.

"Joaquin, what's gotten *into* you? Have you lost your mind?" Though their companions were out of earshot, Han whispered. But loudly.

"Han, you saw what they did to Lyla—"

"Yes, and it was a horrible, horrible thing, but you also saw what I just saw. This is *way* bigger than Lyla, or you, or me. It's way bigger than Natasha and Adler, who are in over their heads. At best, going back will get us martyred in a public square. At worst, they lock us up, throw away the key, and no one ever speaks our names again."

"I can't just sit here—"

"Think of Lyla. Will they treat her better or worse if you do this?"

Joaquin stood up. "Han, are you so blind? If Natasha fails, Lyla's mother's life will be in danger—and, I can tell you, that puts Lyla's life in danger. If we succeed then they'll be safe—and the people of Haline might have a chance." Joaquin exhaled, "My uncle would want us to fight. He knew this would eventually happen."

Joaquin's mind went back to that day with his uncle, that last day, and he recited to Han from memory: "It goes back to the earliest civilizations, this cycle of resource-hungry empires being born, expanding, and dying. It's in our nature, which means it will happen again. We know so little of life outside of our city. Why? We are not past history. We are not immune from its wrath of patterns."

There was a pause, and Joaquin lowered his head. "I'm sorry. It's just that…"

Joaquin sat next to Han. "You're right, this isn't just about Lyla. But it isn't just about revenge either. This is about doing the right thing. Han, the four or five of us may be the only hope the people of this Haline have at not only preserving what little we have left, but turning things around. If what we just heard is even remotely true, President Jemmer is nothing like the man we all believe him to be. He's a pawn, and pawns can be played."

Han sat there looking at his friend. "You don't think staying here, with Rylan and his well-armed and well-fed soldiers, we'll stand a better chance of fighting that fight some other day?"

"Rylan is a good man, but he is an old man. He's a veteran, not a soldier. No…" Joaquin shook his head, "I don't think staying here we stand a better chance. I believe in Natasha, and right now she needs you—and I need you—to help us."

Han held Joaquin's eyes, then turned to look through the open cockpit door. "I was going to be promoted in a couple months, you know." He shook his head, and Joaquin smiled.

"Thank you."

"I'm not doing this for you. Or for Natasha. I'm doing it because you're right, staying here with Rylan I'd get bored out of my mind. I doubt they have much here that would keep life...interesting." Han finally smiled. "Let's do this."

They called Natasha, Adler, and Aaren back, and everyone strapped in for the journey home. There was an energy of possibility and purpose in each of their hearts as they pushed out of their minds questions about what might be to focus on what certainly was.

"Han, how confident are you that you can hack a terminal with a carrier signal?" She sat in the back again with her team.

"Ninety-five percent, Natasha."

As the speeder lifted off the ground Natasha spoke to the cockpit. "Aaren, take us to the west plaza in Gamma."

"All right, heading there now. ETA twenty-one minutes."

**

Aaren punched in his Alpha 2 Class access code to open up Delta gate. He had been told that his clearance level allowed him SAI-blind gate privileges and he prayed he had not been misled. As the massive doors opened he kept a wary eye on the gun turrets trained directly on his craft. He didn't breathe until the speeder safely passed through and the gate closed behind them without incident.

"Natasha, we're about ten minutes away from the plaza. I'm going to have to drop you off about half a mile to the west, and you'll have to foot it from there. Now that we're back in Haline it's only a matter of time until—"

The speeder shook with a violent thud rocking its passengers in their seats, their seatbelts straining against their hips and chests to keep them in place. The lights dimmed and an alarm went off as the speeder decelerated quickly and spun to a standstill, hovering one inch above the ground. Before Aaren or his passengers could ask the question, they had their answer.

"Aaren, this is your chief. You and your passengers are under arrest. Put any and all weapons down and open the speeder door, son. If you comply and come willingly I'll do what I can to commute your pending death sentence."

In an air of slow disbelief Aaren unstrapped himself and turned to face his passengers. The look on his face was sadder than Natasha had expected. The look on Natasha's face was calmer than Aaren believed was warranted, given his confidence about what would happen next.

"I'm sorry." The words were an apology for everything, but most importantly, the executions that likely awaited them. He should never have agreed to bring them back. "I thought...I'm sorry."

Natasha unbuckled herself, stood, and looked at Adler, then Joaquin, then Han. "If anyone should be apologizing it's me. It was my idea to come back. It doesn't matter now.

Guys…" She put her left hand on Joaquin's shoulder and her right on Han's.

"I'll do everything I can to get you out of this. You are and have been our prisoners and did none of this willingly. Do not contradict me out there, please."

There was a sharp knock on the speeder door. "Jemmer, you and the exiles have twenty seconds to come out with your arms raised, or I will use force."

Natasha gave everyone a last look. "Let's go."

She opened the speeder door and walked out, her hands on the back of her head. Adler followed, and then Joaquin, then Han. Aaren dithered, wondering if he had any other options. A moment later, he joined his passengers with his knees on the ground. His arms were pulled behind his back as he was cuffed.

"My orders are to transport you all to Central Square. The president intends to make an example of you, giving you front row seats to watch the Election results come in, making sure every citizen in Haline sees the spectacle. Aaren…" The chief walked from where he was standing in front of the group over to his lieutenant and put a hand on his shoulder.

"I'm incredibly disappointed in you, son. When the president patched me to tell me what he believed you had done I defended you. But you've proven him right and me wrong." The chief paused. "I'm sorry to have to treat you this way. More than that though, I'm sorry you let me down."

The chief glared into Aaren's eyes searching for a

reason for such unexpected officer behavior, finding the familiar eyes of an emboldened serviceman staring back.

"One more thing." The chief searched Aaren's eyes a moment longer then stepped back from him and resumed his position in front of the group. "Your friends out in the mountains are about to pay their price for providing you assistance. As we speak, fighters are en route to their location. They will not survive the hour. We have been aware of their location for some time, but the president had chosen to leave them alone in case they could prove useful in any renewed border skirmishes with Latmero. Today, they sacrificed that opportunity."

The chief scanned their faces, disappointed in the whole situation. "Let's move."

**

> What you're seeing now is Central Square, where some ten thousand Haline citizens are watching the live results along with the president and select members of his cabinet. The viewing stands were erected in just the past four days, a new addition this Election year, as the president wanted to invite key supporters and friends to join in the process and excitement of Election Day.

With half her mind, Natasha lazily watched the HN coverage on the screen in the officer-transport cabin. The rest of her mind turned over the square in her head, exploring any aspect that seemed like an opportunity to disrupt the event. *If they don't chain my feet I can jump from*

my seat and make a run for a broadcast camera. If the path
we walk to our seats comes close to a terminal I can hack a
broadcast until I'm pulled away. If...

Nothing really sounded like a good idea.

"We're here." The voice came through the intercom just as the transport cruised to a stop. The bay door opened and the man behind the voice eyed his prisoners.

"You brought this upon yourselves."

Natasha kept silent, her eyes saying everything she wanted to say.

"It's time to move." The officer in charge of watching them during their short journey pushed Adler to his feet and out the door. Han followed, then Joaquin, then Natasha. Aaren hesitated under the chief's piercing gaze.

"Aaren, it makes me look bad to walk you out in handcuffs, so I'm taking yours off." The chief swiped his finger over Aaren's cuffs, unlocking them and letting them fall to a clang on the floor.

"But know that if you deviate an *inch* from where I tell you to go, I will not hesitate to kill you in front of the world. Do I make myself clear?"

"Yes, sir." Aaren's expression remained unchanged, but he felt himself relax a bit. Handcuffs reminded him of his training days, back when he lived in constant fear of being discovered as a regular. Knowing what he knew now about his parents gave him the comfort of an explanation, but decades of conditioning were hard to break.

Four officers stepped toward them, one behind each of the group, guns pointed squarely into their backs. Natasha dismissed all the bad ideas she'd contemplated...there was zero room to maneuver. She would be dead the moment she so far as leaned out of line.

To Joaquin's surprise the chief had not misled them; they were in fact state guests, and they continued to walk closer and closer to the president's box until they were finally seated front row, just a stone's throw from their adversary. *If only I had a really big stone*, was the only thought that Joaquin had as he sat before turning his eyes to the four massive screens in the middle of the square, one facing each side of the stands. Off to one side in the most central part of the square was a podium where soon the president would remark on early results and seal his victory over the Cotters...and him.

Two of the four attending officers walked back up the steps, leaving one on Joaquin's left and one on Adler's right. To Adler's left sat Aaren, then Han, then Natasha, then Joaquin. The sun burned into their eyes and faces, reminding each of them they were not wearing any protection. Only Aaren was unaffected, as he had not only started his early morning applying officer-class sunblock, but he had also been allowed to keep his dashglass, which cut the glare.

The crowd hummed with the loud buzz of conversation. Some watched the HN broadcast on the screens, but most chatted with their neighbors and friends; to be in the stands was to be in the president's favor—and that was reason to rejoice.

Natasha closed her eyes and inhaled, shutting out the noise and the heat and the smells and focusing on creating options.

"You okay?" Joaquin's voice brought Natasha out of her trance.

"Yeah, just…trying to think of a plan."

"A plan! For what?" Han laughed mockingly and shook his head. "A plan…"

The crowd rose to its feet and erupted in applause as President Gaven Jemmer left the presidential box and walked confidently toward the shielded podium structure at the center of Central Square. He waved as he moved his gaze across the crowd. As his eyes found Natasha and her companions, he offered a condescending salute and a knowing smile. The president reached the podium and waited for the crowd to quiet down and be seated.

"My fellow Halinites. As you can see," Gaven turned to the screen behind him to see the most recent numbers, "it looks like it's going to be a great morning."

Ten thousand citizens stood again and vigorously clapped their hands in early celebration.

"With the polls open only about three hours we already have over forty-five percent of our citizens demanding three more years of progress. Three more years of safety. Three more years of growth. My friends, Halinites across the six

Rings are demanding three more years of this administration, which they trust to deliver on each of these demands, and much more."

The Alphas and Betas were beside themselves, back on their feet and patting each other on the back as if they were winning the Election. In a way, they were.

Natasha finally looked up from her feet where she had been staring in absent thought and squinted in the sun. She instinctively turned her head to shield her eyes and found her gaze fall on Aaren's dashglass. Her eyes widened.

"Han!" Natasha leaned as close to Han as she dared and whispered below the president's booming, magnified voice.

"Yeah?" Han casually turned an ear, captivated by the president, who continued playing the crowd.

"Do you know how to hack an officer-class dashglass to broadcast?"

"Huh? Sure, maybe..." Han was only half listening, still focused on the president's speech.

"Han, listen to me." Natasha whispered with authority.

Han turned his head to face her. "Yes, sorry, what is it, Natasha?"

"Can you hack an officer-class dashglass to broadcast a signal?"

Han turned his head back to the president. "Yeah, it's not even a hack. It's a feat—oh my God!" The lightning that flashed in Han's mind reflected in Natasha's eyes as Han's head spun back around.

"Yes, yes I could do it! But what would you broadcast? No one is going to hear you in the noise, and if you say anything while the presid—"

"Don't worry about that right now. Just set it to broadcast. Think you can do it behind your back? In handcuffs?"

Han turned back to the president with a blank look on his face. In his excitement he had forgotten about that minor detail. "I can try."

"You can do it."

Natasha whispered louder past Han to Aaren. "Aaren, we need to borrow your dashglass. Can you place it in Han's hands? Behind his back?"

Aaren looked confused, and while a thousand questions sprang to mind he realized he was better off not asking any of them; the less he knew, the less conflicted he would feel. Aaren casually took off his dashglass and reached back behind his chair with his left hand. The officer to the left of Joaquin turned to see what the movement was about and was greeted by a blank stare from Aaren as if he were looking out past him, into the crowd to the right of the officer. Aaren held the gaze, offered a curious look, and when the officer turned to follow his eyes Aaren peeked over his shoulder to place the device into Han's hands before turning back to face the president.

Han turned the dashglass in his hands, running his fingers over the arms until he found what he was looking for—a latch where the arm met the frame. Using his thumb he flipped the latch open, exposing an input jack for a hard line and a reset button. Praying that the reset process wouldn't make any noise, he held the button until he felt the dashglass vibrate; letting go, Han powered it down. Running his fingers across to the other elbow of the frame, he depressed the selection button while pushing the reset button, which forced the device to reboot.

The dashglass vibrated again as it sprang back to life, and Han again pushed the selection button. If memory served—and it had been eight months since he had updated the communications protocol on an officer-class dashglass—two taps on the frame would set it to emergency-broadcast mode. Designed as a "last resort," it allowed an officer in danger to broadcast their field of vision to any officers in range should someone be close enough to assist. The hard reset had wiped the "officer only" preset. Now any transceiver, dashglass, or screen would pick up the broadcast.

"They are ready. You just have to trigger the setting." Han kept his eyes on the president, his face expressionless.

"Okay, does Aaren know how it should work?" Natasha, too, looked forward.

"He should. Two taps on the frame. Emergency broadcast is a standard option on an officer-class dashglass."

Natasha leaned slightly to her right. "Aaren, we need you to put your dashglass back on. When I say the word, trigger the broadcast setting."

"I removed the officer-only encoding, so…" Han let Aaren's imagination take it from there.

"I'm not going to do it, Natasha." Aaren reached behind Han, grabbed his dashglass, and casually put it back on. "If you can take these off of me you can use them as you see fit, but I won't be complicit in your plans."

"When the time is right you'll make the right decision." Natasha stared ahead, a gleam of hope in her eyes. "And it will be obvious when that time comes."

**

"In a minute, I'm going to let Congressional Leader Danyela Clarek say a few words—now, now, please be respectful." Hundreds in the crowd had booed, just as Gaven had hoped.

"While it's true that Congress and I have been disagreeing a fair amount as of late, I have a lot of respect for Danyela and thank her for being here to support me. She and select other members of Congress are aware that the status quo is dysfunctional and in need of overhaul. I commend Danyela on her hard work to control some of the more, shall we say, radical members of Congress. Danyela?"

Danyela Jymar Clarek stood awkwardly a moment in front of her chair, scanning the twenty thousand eyes in the stands fixated on her. For the first time in as long as she could remember, she felt nervous.

"Danyela." The president repeated her name, this time

less of a question and more of a command. Danyela snapped out of her daze and moved to the podium to scattered applause in the audience that barely lasted the length of her walk.

"Thank you, Mr. President." Danyela greeted Gaven with deference on her face, in her voice, and through her stature before looking down at the ground. She inhaled then turned to face the microphone and stood a moment before lifting her eyes to the HN camera ahead of her.

"Mr. President, distinguished guests, and my fellow Halinites. For the past six years I have led our Congress in working for the people, at times in agreement with the president and other times in discord with his policies and opinions."

The left corner of the president's mouth lifted ever so slightly. The audience had quieted to less than a whisper. Joaquin had moved to the edge of his seat, an inexplicable discomfort growing within him as he watched Lyla's mother.

"But over the past several months as I've seen our Congress fail to serve its people, and over the past several hours as I've seen those same people reaffirm their unwavering faith in our president..."

Natasha's jaw fell open. Joaquin's clamped shut and through his teeth in a deep and toxic growl he muttered, "They still have Lyla. They must."

"I have come to realize Congress no longer represents the people who elected us, and most importantly, who elected me. A Congress that doesn't represent the views of its people is not a Congress in which I wish to serve. And so today, Haline's third Election Day, I'm resigning as congressional leader."

She paused a half second, finished with a "Thank you," and turned from the microphone. Danyela Clarek was halfway back to her seat before her words had sunk in for the crowd, but by the time she was seated it had erupted into a chant—"Jemmer! Jemmer! Jemmer!"

The president, his face a look of feigned surprise, waved the crowd into quiet.

"Danyela." He looked in her direction and shook his head and then turned to the audience. "That was unexpected. While I'm of course saddened by Danyela Clarek's decision to resign, I must admit I am not surprised. As a loyal public servant she only seeks to serve her people, and today the people of Haline are unequivocally choosing progress over bureaucracy and agreement over dispute."

He turned in the former congressional leader's direction. "Danyela, I thank you for your service." The president's gaze then moved to Natasha and her companions, and he smiled.

20

"Friends and fellow citizens, before we continue let's pledge our allegiance to Haline. All rise and salute." As the Haline flag with its six red rings and blocky *H* was hoisted up the pole mid-distance between the podium and the audience, people began getting up from their seats. The president took a step back from the podium and saluted.

The officers to Joaquin's left and Adler's right moved behind their prisoners. Running their fingers over the handcuffs, they removed them one by one. The officer to Joaquin's left whispered loudly so all could hear him: "The president has ordered you to stand and salute the flag. If you do not comply, you will be stunned, removed, and placed into solitary confinement until charged."

Natasha managed a smile as she rubbed her hands over her sore wrists and stood up. "It's okay guys...we all *are* loyal to Haline, are we not? Let the president get his footage." Her right hand moved to the top right of her forehead in salute.

"Aaren." Natasha stared forward but leaned toward Aaren with a whisper. "You'll forgive me if I take your dashglass from you after the pledge."

His head quickly turned to her then back to the flag. "To broadcast what, Natasha? And will it really work? Look," he leaned slightly in her direction, speaking across Han, "I can try to convince the president to reduce your sentence to exile. Knowing what we know now..." Aaren paused. "I'm just not sure it's worth you risking your life at this point."

Natasha stared ahead but leaned toward Aaren and spoke in quiet confidence. "I have no choice, Aaren."

Aaren's face tensed with defeat as he realized there was no convincing her otherwise. Natasha intended to alter the outcome of this Election or die trying.

Natasha turned to her left to look at Joaquin with soft eyes and saw his newfound anger etched into lines on his face, his gaze fixated on the flag, his mouth sewn shut. She lingered there a moment before swiveling her head 180 degrees to look upon Adler. He too was focused on the flag, but recited the pledge with the love of a wounded but ever-loyal fighter. She hoped he would approve of what she was about to do.

Closing her eyes, she inhaled, ran over her one-sentence speech one last time, and exhaled. It was short—she hoped short enough that she could make it all the way through. The crowd had moved to singing the anthem, and Natasha opened her eyes and spoke to Aaren in a loud whisper, "I'm sorry if this hurts you."

"Natasha, look!" Han's excited tone broke Natasha's concentration, and she followed his eyes out to the horizon. On fast approach were three dots that must have been ships of some kind. The pledge finished and people began taking their seats, but some remained standing and stared out into the distance. Slowly the dots resolved into three officer-class transports.

Alpha was a no-fly zone—even for SAI scouts—and the sight of the approaching transports had more and more people whispering and pointing. Many began assuming they were in for some sort of show or surprise; perhaps the president had arranged something special to celebrate his whopping showing at the polls and pending eighty-percent-of-the-electorate victory?

It was just as he was about to resume his speech that the president himself heard the hum of distant engines from behind him and turned. A second later he was darting from the podium toward the presidential box, screaming orders to his Citizen Guard to open fire.

CG forces on the ground fanned out, took positions across the square, and fired up at the approaching transports. Arriving in a stealth formation, what appeared to be three ships were in fact six, and they split into six directions around the square. Hatches opened and gunfire was returned, the crowd now screaming and ducking under their seats or trampling over each other to escape the firefight.

The single squadron of officers stationed at various checkpoints around the square were paralyzed in confusion as the approaching transports bore Haline Police markings. Hesitant to fire on what appeared to be their own, they all patched into command asking for their orders. Haline Police Chief Trey Benlin sat staring as if he'd seen a ghost, his mouth ajar, ignoring his transceiver.

One of the transports bellowed black smoke and began spiraling, dropping several hundred feet behind the stands and exploding into a fireball that flashed brighter than the sun. Seconds later the other five successfully landed on the green of the square and officers began pouring out—guns firing on the Citizen Guard soldiers who were holding their ground.

The president had reached his bulletproof, bombproof box and frantically tried to assess the situation, wholly confused by what was happening. His first guess as he ran from the podium was that Venka had ordered the attack and wondered if (prayed!) it was part of some staged assassination attempt to bolster his support. He grabbed the closest portable screen and began configuring it for secure communication—then he looked up and realized it wasn't staged at all and worse than he could have possibly imagined.

As the last Citizen Guard soldier on the field fell and the newly landed officers secured the square, one figure took off his officer helmet and put it under his arm as he walked out from behind the protection of his transport toward the president's box.

"Rylan." It was more a growl than a name, a word, or a sentence.

The president dropped the screen from his hands and reached for both his guns, ran to the nearest shielded gun turret, and in a blind passion opened fire in Rylan's direction with a scream louder than the rapidly firing bullets.

The helmet dropping from his hands, Rylan ducked and rolled toward the podium a dozen feet away. There, he cowered until he realized the bullets intended for him were harmlessly ricocheting off the glass. He slowly stood behind the podium's protection with defiant eyes toward Gaven.

In a flash, the president stopped firing as a thought stuck him—*HN was still broadcasting across Haline!* He looked up at the screens for the latest Election results and saw to his horror the unfolding scene live with the headline: "Assassination Attempt at Central Square."

"Gaven…" Rylan stopped as he heard his whisper magnified twenty times and turned to see a microphone embedded into the podium. His heart skipped a beat, and he turned to face the crowd, his hands gripping the podium by both sides.

"My fellow countrymen, it's Rylan, your faithful soldier who was double-crossed into exile. It's been a long seven years, but I've come here today to stop this puppet of a man from clinching a victory he did not earn and that he will abuse if granted. He does not serve you, but—"

The microphone cut out, as did all the screens around the stands. Rylan's head whipped toward the president's booth to see a fresh squadron of Citizen Guard fighters spring out in his direction. His soldier instinct sent him running back to the closest transport as behind him guns were drawn and shots were fired. Ahead of him, Rylan saw Matthias and his troops returning fire—and then a sharp pain radiated out from his right shoulder. He fought to keep his balance, fumbling forward onto the ground.

"Nooo!" Matthias grabbed a minmax shield and ran the ten feet out to Rylan, gripped his left arm, and pulled him into safety behind the transport—all the while firing out on the oncoming soldiers.

Several of the Citizen Guard reached the podium case, pushed it over onto its side, and took position behind it, firing at the scattering officers who ran from transport to transport in search of an attack angle.

**

"Rylan!" Natasha couldn't contain her emotion when she saw him go down. Natasha, Joaquin, Adler, Han, and Aaren had been cowering in paralyzed awe while the stands around them emptied, everyone fleeing from the fighting. Officers still crouched at either side of them, and though their hands were uncuffed Natasha was wary to risk action, the chief's words running through her mind. If he was ready to shoot his own lieutenant in front of the world, he would not hesitate to take down the head of the Cotters or her companions—and he still sat just twenty feet away above the president's box.

"What does this mean?" Standing there during the pledge, Aaren was overcome by his deep love for Haline, a people and place that he had spent almost his whole life fighting to serve and protect. He had no family or friends, so Haline and its people had become his life companions. But upon understanding Natasha's determination to sacrifice her own life in her own way of service to those same people and that same place, his love felt...empty. Which Haline did he serve? Which did he love?

When he saw Rylan standing defiantly at the podium appealing to the people, Aaren felt the man was speaking directly to him. He repeated the question emphatically, turning his head toward Natasha. "Natasha, what does this mean?"

"I don't know..." She shook her head and then turned to Aaren, "but you have a choice to make, Aaren. You can stand by as an officer waiting to be sentenced, or you can help us stop the president and reclaim our country for its people— and honor the sacrifice your parents made all those years ago."

She paused. "If I take your dashglass, set it to broadcast, and stand up—I'll be shot within seconds. But you...Aaren, you can serve your people by showing them what's happening here, right now. People across Haline think this is just an assassination attempt and are likely to gather around the president in solidarity after it's all over. You can show them that their faith is misplaced by broadcasting what's really happening here in Central Square. That Patriots have returned to fight on their behalf. For their future."

Aaren stared out at the Citizen Guard advancing on the officers, then turned to look at his chief, who despite everything unfolding in front of him had barely blinked, then at the remaining Alphas and Betas in the stands scrambling to escape. If a broadcast was going to have any effect it would have to start now. And it would have to last longer than the few seconds Natasha would last.

**

"Gimme everyone, now! I'm under attack, you useless idiot! *Now!*" The president hung up with his Citizen Guard lieutenant back at Bunker One and was about to get his police chief on the line, when he noticed the darkened central screens flash to life out of the corner of his eye. Turning his head, he saw in panic a live broadcast of the firefight in the square.

The president opened a line to HN HQ. "Wilden! I told you to cut Central Square broadcast. Why the hell am I seeing it back up on the screen?"

"Mr. President, our team on the ground confirms suspended broadcast. It's not them, sir! And I don't see broadcast on any of the channels here...whatever you're seeing must be local."

"What?! What do you mean local…" Within his box, the president took a few steps to his right to get a better view of the screen and realized the point of view was not from HN cameras. He ran out to the edge of his box and saw Aaren standing, his left hand on his dashglass. The president turned his head back to the screens, then back to Aaren, then back to the screens, then back to Aaren. "Son of a *bitch*! SAI, I need a dozen scouts to my present location, now!"

"Mr. President, you are in a no-fly zone. Scouts are not authorized."

"Override, dammit! Presidential access code Charlie, Delta, Delta, Two, One, Four, Alpha, Six, Six."

"Your override authority has been suspended." President Gaven Jemmer froze, contemplating the implications. *The Board means to abandon me!*

Grunting while holstering his guns, Gaven unzipped his inner jacket pocket and grabbed his OCD—a small device that emitted a hypersonic pulse audible only to genetically enhanced officers. The president put it around his left wrist, set it to fire in ten seconds, and ran out of his protected box toward Aaren.

"Aaren, thank goodness you have broadcast ability! The enemy cut our HN coverage, and the people of Haline need to know of this bold atrocity in Central Square—"

"Ahhhhh!" A scream erupted from in front of the president, but three people down from his target. Joaquin's hands tightly covered his ears as he doubled over in pain.

Turning his head from a screaming Joaquin, Aaren saw a blinking device attached behind the president's left wrist. Aaren turned and reached into the holster of the doubled-over officer to his right, whose hands were also desperately covering his ears, grabbed his gun, and pointed it in the president's direction.

"Shut that device off, *now*!"

"Aaren, no!" Natasha's head whirled from Joaquin to the gun pointed at Gaven Jemmer and her hand shot out to push it down. "You can't fire on Gaven!"

"Ahhhh!" Joaquin wailed in pain, and Natasha's head turned back to his agony.

"Arggh!" Aaren holstered the gun and leapt from his seat onto the field, tackling the president and ripping the device off his wrist. They both landed hard, and Aaren immediately rolled over and crushed the device with his fist—only then feeling a sharp pain flood his upper chest. Looking down, Aaren saw an expanding red patch on his clothes where his minmax vest usually sat, suddenly remembering the Guard soldier he saw out the corner of his eye as he sailed through the air toward the president. Fighting to contain the pain, Aaren turned his head and saw that same Guard soldier running in his direction, gun drawn—forgetting for the moment that what he saw, everyone saw, as his intact dashglass continued to broadcast.

Joaquin's hands came off his ears and he sat panting in sweat, slowly regaining his breath.

"What the..." Joaquin looked up at Natasha, his eyes blurry with tears.

"Are you okay?" Seeing his agony lift, Natasha's arms spread out around Joaquin in a tight embrace.

"I...what the hell was that?"

"I have an idea, but there's no time to explain. We have to—Aaren!" Turning her head from Joaquin to look out at the square, Natasha saw Aaren immobile and bleeding on the ground. Three Citizen Guard soldiers ran in his direction, two with guns drawn as the president slowly stood back up a few feet away.

Joaquin raised his head, and seeing one of the Citizen Guards pause to take aim at Aaren, he jumped to his feet. He turned to the recovering officer at his left, took his gun from its holster, shot the officer in the foot, and then turned and opened fire at the oncoming soldiers. Two guards fell instantly, and the third jumped to protect the president. Joaquin leapt onto the field to pull Aaren back into the relative safety of the stands.

The president made a break back to his box and the third Guard soldier followed him, but two Guard soldiers approached from across the square to address the new threat.

"Joaquin! Behind you!" Natasha scrambled to the wounded officer, and before he knew what was happening she reached over him and pulled out the backup gun from around his calf.

"Ahhh!" Joaquin had spun around and opened fire on the approaching guards, taking out the closer soldier, but the one farther from him fired a clean shot at Joaquin's right arm, and the gun dropped from his hand as he fell to his knees, the stun reverberating through his body. The soldier continued his advance on Joaquin and, seeing no backup to support an arrest, raised his gun to finish him off.

Joaquin straightened his back and inhaled, closed his eyes, and prepared for the shot. He heard it fire and his body shuddered—but seconds passed without the expected sharp pain. Opening his eyes, he saw the soldier fall to his knees and then to the ground. Joaquin struggled to his feet using his left hand, turned, and saw Natasha frozen—a gun in both hands.

"Natasha…" Joaquin felt emotion rise up from his core into his chest and moisten his eyes.

Natasha stared at the gun as she lowered it, panting. She looked up at the soldier who now lay motionless on the ground, back at the gun, and up at the soldier. And then she saw Joaquin standing and she calmed. Placing the gun in her holster she leapt over the divider and embraced him, looking at the wound.

"I'll be fine." Joaquin's voice was normal, and Natasha saw in his eyes that he meant his words.

"Joaquin…" Aaren's breathing had become erratic, but

his mind calmed as he experienced his epiphany. He looked up, a pleading note to his voice. "Thank you, Joaquin. For taking my place."

Lying there, Aaren had had time to understand what Natasha understood the moment Joaquin doubled over in pain and what slowly dawned on Joaquin as they stood there now. Alyel and Soel had not somehow added their child to the officer nursery, but had replaced a newborn with their own. They had swapped their only son, Aaren, for the parentless government property that was Joaquin. The irony of it as he lay there in pain brought a smile to his face, and he coughed a laugh through his tears.

"No, Aaren..." Joaquin kneeled and took Aaren's right hand into his left. "Thank you...for taking mine."

Adler had jumped over the divider and was applying to Aaren what first-aid care he could, attempting to stop the bleeding—but knowing it to be an impossible task. Aaren drifted unconscious, and Adler moved to attempt resuscitation.

"Aaren!" Natasha fell to her knees and took Aaren's other hand while Adler worked on reviving him. The third thump to his chest opened Aaren's eyes to Natasha. He strained his head around toward Joaquin, and amid desperate, wheezing breaths, he lips in a smile, he opened his mouth as if to form a word—and then his neck stiffened and his eyes glazed.

Natasha caught a sob in her throat with a hand that

shot to her mouth, while Adler, Joaquin, and Han were each hit by a pain in their chest. A stray bullet sailed into the divider a few feet down, momentarily pulling them all out from their anguish to survey the battlefield.

"Guys, look..." Han leaned over the divider and pointed up at the screens. The HN crew had finally blocked the signal from Aaren's dashglass and replaced it with Election result coverage, but the damage had been done. To any viewer, it was obvious that the president had tried to immobilize the officer wearing the broadcasting dashglass—and so had something to hide. As word spread across Haline, voting had slowed to a standstill. The people waited anxiously for updates on what was really happening at Central Square.

Safe in his box as the fighting continued outside between his Guard and Rylan's soldiers, the president sat with his head in his hands.

21

In a heavy silence broken only by scattered gunfire behind them, Natasha, Adler, and Han lifted Aaren's limp body over the divider between the stands and the battlefield and set it down across the seats before ducking down next to it. Joaquin rolled over the barrier and crouched, more tired than he'd ever felt in his whole life.

Natasha knew she had to be the first to say something. Her emotions rolled from grief, to fear, to anger, and back to grief. But she still had to lead.

"I don't know why the Haline officers aren't taking sides, but if they stay neutral I think Rylan's men have the Guard outnumbered. Adler and I will do what we can. Han, you stay here with Joaquin and…Aaren. Take this." She removed her gun from its holster. "I'm not going to need it."

"Natasha." Despite the loss of blood, Joaquin's voice was strong.

"If anything happens to us, it's on you two to make sure

Rylan knows what Officer Aaren Jemmer did here today."
Natasha's voice was equally firm as she ignored him. Han
took the gun from her hand, and she was about to stand
when the hum of a drone turned her head to the sky just in
time to catch the transceiver it was dropping.

"Natasha! Can you hear me?"

She eyed Adler as she put the transceiver on.

"Yes…Rylan?

"Yes, thank God you're alive. I saw Gaven and his men
in your vicinity and feared the worst."

"We lost Aaren." She spoke quicker than she felt the
gravity of the situation deserved. "Joaquin is wounded, but
stable."

"I'm sorry." Rylan's pause of respectful silence was
short. "Listen, stay put. I'll send a team over there to escort
you to medical as soon as I can. Another five, ten minutes
tops. Can you hold your position?"

Natasha looked at her companions with as much hope
as she dared reveal lest she raise expectations more than she
should. "Yeah, we'll be here."

"Good. We have most of his men cornered. This should
all be over soon."

"Rylan, how did you—"

"The datacard I gave you. Besides the map it had a mic.
I needed to know how you would handle…well, handle
everything. The moment your speeder was hit we feared the
worst, not only for you but for us. Wait a second." Rylan

went quiet, leaving Natasha wondering.

"Back. Matthias already had everyone suited up and ready. Somehow he knew today was the day. Smart kid."

"I saw you go down."

"Flesh wound. Okay, more than a flesh wound, but medical says I'll be fine. Wait one second, Natasha."

Natasha lifted her eyes to Adler, Joaquin, and Han. "They're sending a team."

"Natasha, I have to go. I should see you here in about twenty minutes."

"Okay...wait, one last thing." Natasha closed her eyes.

"Yes?"

"Gaven...does he know...what you told me?"

"I don't know, Natasha. It's very possible he does not."

"Okay." For some reason, she found the news a relief. She opened her eyes and removed the transceiver.

"What was that about?" Joaquin inquired in a mixture of suspicion and concern.

"Nothing. Let's get ready to move quickly as soon as Rylan's men get here."

**

"My God, Vee. I couldn't! It was Rylan! How did you expect me to fire on *Rylan*?" The chief held his ground, his face sweaty and red and defensive.

"So you just stood aside while he fired on your president?" Gaven was working to keep his voice down, but the desperation was audible to anyone passing by.

"Don't give me that line, Vee." The chief pulled in close, lowering his voice to a whisper. "None of his men fired a shot in your direction. And what about the fact that you lied to me? I suspected it was him in those mountains, but you gave me your word that it wasn't."

The chief shook his head. "I would have had his blood on my hands if our assault this morning had succeeded. You should have told me."

Gaven Jemmer, President of Haline, hung his head in defeat. He wanted to blame everything on his police chief, but deep down he knew the fault was his own. He turned to walk away but saw Rylan approaching. Behind Rylan in a circle sat what was left of his Citizen Guard, their hands cuffed behind their backs.

"Gentlemen, I hope I'm not interrupting anything." Rylan's right arm hung in a sling, but he walked with the authority of a victorious leader. He moved from Gaven Jemmer's conflicted gaze to Trey's eyes, which filled with as much admiration and affection as a hardened army colonel turned police chief could effuse.

"We were just wondering what happens now." While it wasn't exactly what they had been discussing, Trey knew it was the only question worth asking.

"Jemmer." Rylan put his left hand on Gaven's right shoulder. "You have a choice."

Rylan paused to look around the square, his hand still on the president's shoulder, and together their eyes surveyed the scene. Nearly empty stands where ten thousand had stood just an hour before. Blood stains and bullet holes marked what had been the only manicured green field in all of Haline. Men and women in constrained agony and pain being tended to by nurses and doctors, some being evacuated to the military hospital near Bunker One, a row of bodies for whom care was too late close by. Natasha, Joaquin, and Adler sitting by their fallen enemy turned savior, Aaren. Rylan returned his eyes to Jemmer's.

"You have a choice." Rylan repeated. "Side with The Board or side with your people." His hand fell from Jemmer's shoulder as he took a step closer and lowered his voice.

"Neither choice will be easy." He let a moment pass. "Side with The Board and I'll exile you as you once exiled me, leaving you to their mercy. What's left of your conscience will eat at you for the rest of your life as you abandon the very people you fought to save, serve, and protect the last twenty years of your life. Your parents...well, you would betray everything they ever stood for." Rylan was careful not to mention that Gaven had already betrayed his parents; he needed Gaven to think this was his chance at redemption. As much as he didn't want to admit it, he needed Gaven.

"Or. Side with your people. With me. And let's continue what we started together before Venka, before The Board, before Haline. It will be the biggest challenge of your life, but it will be worth it. And we will win."

Gaven whipped his head around to face Rylan directly.

"We will *not* win, Rylan. You have no idea what you're up against."

"I've seen—"

"You've seen nothing!" Gaven stepped back, taking a breath to calm the fierce conflict that ripped at his insides.

"Gentlemen, we have a more urgent issue. The polls are still open but voting has completely stopped." Trey broke the stalemate. "Rylan, the people of Haline need to know what's going on. There hasn't been an incident of this magnitude since the wars. We must contain it quickly." The chief nodded his head toward the screens at the center of the square where the vote count stood nearly frozen.

The president didn't bother looking. He knew what he would see—reality. And failure. Instead he stared past his feet. *If I choose exile I won't last a day. They'd have me killed and position Ginara to become president.* He shook his head at the thought of his vice president succeeding him. *If I stay, The Board will have us all killed—unless I can convince Rylan to let me continue to lead and The Board that I have everything under control.*

He shook his head ever so slightly. *How do I convince Rylan to trust me?* He sighed in frustration when a spark returned to his dead eyes as he was struck with a thought. He looked back up at Rylan.

"I'm with the people. *And* The Board. It doesn't have to be a choice. It can't be. If this government loses an ounce of control, we lose the dream that is Haline—and we're all dead." Before Rylan could argue, Gaven Jemmer left the men and walked briskly to where Natasha stood above Aaren, Joaquin's good arm around her side, their heads low.

"Natasha, I need a word." He moved his eyes around her companions and then returned to her. Natasha took a half step back from him and inhaled, working to shake the emotion of loss that had saturated her completely just seconds before to grasp the frantic president's request.

"What. For." The anger that had been piling at the pit of her chest the past days and months and years seeped into her voice as her defeated foe asked something *he* needed of *her*. But then she saw in the president's eyes something she had never seen before: fear. She inhaled again to contain her emotion. *Now is not the time...not yet.*

"We need to act quickly and address the people. Memories of the violence before Haline are barely six years old, and the people need to understand that what they just saw does not threaten the safety and security we've all worked so hard to build. And I need your help." He motioned his head away from the group. "Walk with me."

Natasha turned to Joaquin, who coldly seethed toward the president; she knew any counsel he might provide would be tainted with vengeance. Her eyes moved to Adler, who shook his head slowly back and forth, deliberately. *No!* His expression was definitive. Han's face was unreadable, but she saw in him the anxiety the president spoke of, likely shared by most citizens across Haline.

"I'll be right back." Natasha looked on each of them with the hint of a forced but comforting smile and then began walking with Gaven toward the center of the field. Gaven subtly activated his soundcatch to ensure their conversation was shielded from SAI.

"You're afraid. Of what?"

"All is not as it seems, Natasha. The suppliers I've spoken of as generous trading partners are—"

"I know about The Board."

"Wha...you know? How? Of course, Rylan must have told you." He grimaced as he spoke his name. "Natasha, if we don't reassure the people of Haline and contain this morning's events, The Board will take action to preserve stability and, I assure you, my administration will be considered gratuitously benevolent compared to what they'd undoubtedly impose."

Natasha walked a moment, pondering. "What do you propose?"

"A press conference where we denounce the assassination attempt by Rylan and his men as remnants of the Resist—"

"*What?* Why would—"

"Let me finish."

Natasha had stopped walking. They were barely out of earshot from the group and she cringed knowing that they likely heard her yelp. *Stay calm.*

Gaven paused to look at her and contemplated showing

her the soundcatch, but then kept walking, expecting her to keep up. She moved forward.

"We publicly denounce the attack. We have to…the fighting they saw today—between my Citizen Guard and what they saw as officers—will be viewed by the people as an attack on everything we stand for. They'll be looking for enduring strength in Haline leadership—in me—to ease doubt and concern. They'll be looking for confidence and resolution."

He paused, his face softening. "But by the same turn they'll need me to acknowledge the root cause of the attack. I will pin it to a loss of balance in the country, and declare a new partnership—with you. I'll make the Cotters an official political party that you will lead in Congress."

The anger she had quieted began burning again. She stopped walking. "Gaven, listen to yourself. You just want to maintain control. As if nothing happened today! Why would Rylan agree to that? Why would I?" Natasha stared at her nemesis of the past six years and wondered how she could ever accept him as anything else.

"Who will lead Haline and protect us from The Board, Natasha? *You*?"

Natasha had never in her wildest dreams imagined the situation she was in. Replacing President Jemmer herself was never something she wanted; her objective had always been policy, not politics.

"What…what about Danyela Clarek? Surely she—"

"She's lost the faith and confidence of the people. Natasha, as long as I'm alive the citizens of Haline will reject anyone else but me. You *need* me to lead."

As much as it pained her to admit it, Natasha realized he was right. Over the past six years Gaven had adroitly positioned himself as the sole beacon of authority in all of Haline. Right now, there was no one else the people would follow. She exhaled defeat and offered a compromise. "Fine, but only if we come clean to the people about The Board and—"

"Impossible! After what happened today, we need to send a signal to The Board that Haline will emerge from this stronger and more stable than she was yesterday or any day since her founding. Anything less and they will take action."

"We could fight." In her mind, she pictured the president as the first prisoner of war, perhaps a prize she could use to bargain with The Board.

"Ha!" Gaven's laugh mismatched his furrowed brow. "Fight? With what? They control everything, Natasha. *Everything.* As it is, they keep us on life support, restricting supplies while they gorge themselves in excess…Natasha, we wouldn't last a week without Board supplies."

Emboldened by the morning's events, Natasha continued defiantly. "Rylan was able to survive in the mountains without Board supplies. There is a way—"

"There is no way, Natasha, that anything can change overnight. If we fight, we'll all be dead within the week."

Natasha opened her mouth to protest but again saw in Gaven's eyes the same fear that had initially given her pause. She turned and looked out at the empty stands, at the red and brown and black and green field of grass, at the seated circle of Guard prisoners, and she then inhaled to clear her mind. *Could we last without Board supplies? Nearly six million people. We'd need time to learn Rylan's methods...*

Perhaps he was right. Perhaps there was no other way. *But I can't stand with him.*

"I won't do it." Natasha shook her head. "Rylan can lead us in Congress."

"Rylan is not who you think he is, Natasha. You've only heard his side of the story, remember that. Besides, The Board wouldn't accept him—but they might accept you. We'll figure out a place for Rylan, but it cannot be prominent. Not after what everyone saw today. For now, he'll need to be publicly exiled back to his mountains."

Gaven saw Natasha about to object. "There's no other alternative, Natasha, and time is short. Right now we both want the same thing—to preserve safety and security and to convince The Board not to retaliate."

He paused and dropped his voice. "Once things settle, we can bring Rylan back and deal with The Board. But for now we need to restore order and the only way we can do that—we being all of us, including Rylan—is if you and I work together."

A thought struck Gaven and his eyebrows lowered, light

again dancing in his eyes. "As brother and sister."

Natasha snapped straight. "So it's true?"

"Yes...how do...of course. Rylan." The name rolled off his tongue like bile.

Natasha felt emotion move into her chest and she willed it still, shaking her head. "I...don't understand. You're Ashten? In my memories, there was..."

She shook her head again, her eyes on her feet. "I have these nightmares..."

"I don't know what to tell you, Natasha. I don't know who Ashten is or what you remember, but for what it's worth I have my own nightmares."

He paused, and Natasha looked up and saw in his eyes something else she had never seen before.

"I do know, however, that you're my sister. Venka told me."

It was almost more than Natasha could bear, this avalanche of revelations. "Rylan mentioned Venka...who is she?"

"She's...a member of The Board. My superior."

Almost more than she could bear. She shook her head. "I can't believe this. Any of this."

Natasha took a step back and stared out at the abandoned stands. Gaven continued: "You know, I wanted to crush you and the rest of the Cotters. And I could have. The only thing that stopped me was knowing that we had the same parents."

"Why would they—"

"Control, Natasha. They knew they'd created a monster in me, and they also knew that they needed to contain the expected dissenters. To manage them. *They* selected you to lead the Cotters. *They* set you up to abhor violence."

Natasha whipped around.

"Yes, Venka told me that too. It became another reason I could never…Natasha, we're wasting time. We can talk about this later, but for now the people are waiting."

"What about the other Halines?"

Gaven's mouth opened but he immediately knew the answer to the question he wanted to ask. Natasha continued. "We saw, Gaven, with our own eyes. Another city, with the same rings, just over the mountains."

Gaven shook his head. "So you understand how important it is for us to stand together, in solidarity, and convince The Board we've contained the situation here. That in a month, the events of today will be a distant memory to the average Halinite. Natasha, right now our job is to preserve and protect *our* Haline. We can worry about the other Halines later—if we survive."

She turned to look back at her comrades and saw them carrying Aaren to a transport. She was struck by a desire to leave Gaven and join them. Wasn't that where she belonged? With her team? "You know, all I wanted was to stop your march toward absolute control. My parents, *our* parents, gave their lives fighting to prevent the last government from achieving absolute control. And now you're asking me to help you maintain that control."

"I've never had control, Natasha. You were never fighting me. You were always fighting The Board. I'm giving you a chance to continue that fight."

She paused, distant. "Why should I trust you?"

"You have no other choice. No one else can peacefully lead Haline *and* avoid the wrath of The Board. Trust me because this also is the only choice *I* have. I can't do this without you." Gaven Jemmer extended a steady hand to a steadfast Natasha.

She stared blankly at the hand and then at the man who owned it, remaining quiet a long moment. Her mind went back to memories of her mother and father, and she closed her eyes to play out her options in her head. In one, she saw suffering and violence and the prospect of a futile death. In the other, she saw only a rough cloud of uncertainty.

Hearing a distant clacking sound, Natasha opened her eyes to the stands, where a brave few Alphas and Betas were beginning to filter back into the square. Slowly two shapes turned into four, then four to a dozen, as their curiosity moved their feet from the stands onto the field. In a flash, her mind moved to the people of the other Halines.

"Gaven...did the other Halines have their Elections today?"

"Yes," he lied.

"And are they...like us?"

"Worse." Again.

Natasha's face turned to Gaven, who had lowered his hand, her mouth saying nothing but her eyes saying enough. Then she returned her gaze to Adler, Joaquin, and Han, who stood by the transport with Aaren's body.

Finally, she replied. "Danyela gets reinstated as Congressional Leader." She paused. "And we'll need to convince Rylan."

Natasha inhaled a long breath and began walking toward her comrades. Gaven Jemmer barely heard her parting words, more an exhale than a sentence—not sure if they were meant for him.

"Our work is not done."

a request

Thank you for reading HALINE.

I wrote the book to describe a possible "post-climate change" future, one that might result if we continue marching down the exploitive path we are on. Unfortunately, climate change is not fiction.

Join us at haline.co where together we can understand the implications of climate change and learn what we can do to make our tomorrow better, today.

special thanks

After I wrote my first draft of HALINE, I turned to friends, family, and the indiegogo community to crowdfund professional editing, cover art, and other parts of the final novel. Over 140 people contributed, and I'd like to give special thanks to the following individuals for their generous support of my campaign, viewable at indiegogo.com/projects/haline:

Aemish Shah	Jamie Chvotkin	Reshma Anvekar
Alex McIntosh	Jennifer H Cipperly	Reza Bavar
Andrew Hoag	Joe Greenstein	Rick Marini
Anh Duong	John Gamero	Robert ONeill
Anil Dindigal	Joshua Newman	Santiago Suarez
Ayesha & Premal Shah	Ken Ebbitt	Satyender Mahajan
Ben Rattray	Kristine Penner Klein	Seema Patel
Bryan Rollins	Lauren Weinstein	Sharat & Shicha Chander
Carrie Feigel Bischke	Maria Wu Kiskis	Sarah Harding
Cliff Wang	Matthew Flannery	Slava Rubin
Dan Lack	Nick Bhatt	Stephan Cesarini
Dan Martell	Nicole Goi	Stephanie Lem
Daniel Rosen	Otis Chandler	Steve Chen
David Kashen	Prashanth Ranganathan	Steven T Puri
Deborah Mullin	Puneet Agarwal	Sunil Daluvoy
Deepa Vora	Raffael Marty	Tia Link
Dhruv Singh	Rahul Khurana	Veer Gidwaney
Eyal Gutentag	Raj Irukulla	Vikram Grover
Ian Johnstone	Ravi Patel	Yrmis Barroeta

9249264R00147

Made in the USA
San Bernardino, CA
10 March 2014